THE LADY IN WHITE

BY DONALD WILLERTON

THE LADY IN WHITE

A MOGI FRANKLIN MYSTERY
BOOK 7

DONALD WILLERTON

WISE WOLF
BOOKS

For My Mother

THE LADY IN WHITE

CHAPTER 1

NORTHEASTERN NEW MEXICO, AUGUST 10, 1870

"Tipton! You need to be up! It's a special day!" Tip Mulvaney hunkered deeper into the cool of his sheets and tried to imagine how a cow might be trained to milk itself. He finally yawned, stretched, and leaned back to watch a ray of sunlight slice across the flowers in the wallpaper across from the window.

He took a deep breath. The best time of the day was early morning, the moisture in the air making even better the smells of the kitchen downstairs. Another hour and the sun would be hot and harsh, drying the air to only a whisper of moisture, and the main smells would be of dust, sage, and juniper trees.

The springs squeaked as he rose from the bed, stretched, slipped on his long-sleeve shirt, and then pulled on his coveralls. The shirt was required: he was a pale-skinned redhead like his father, and the hot summer sun would toast whatever parts of him were showing. He also had to wear a hat to prevent his face from becoming a dense field of freckles. Struggling into boots that already seemed too small, he heard the clanking of pans downstairs.

Father had let the cook go at the beginning of summer.

Mother had taken on the cooking for everyone though some of the ranch hands had been smart and followed the cook. Mother's cooking was getting better, but her early meals had been a challenge some of the hands hadn't survived.

As he did every morning, Tip stood next to the door frame, running his hand from the top of his head as evenly across as he could to the tick marks on the paint. Subtracting off the height of his boots, he was sure there was a little improvement. He moved from the door to the mirror. The image was of a tall, thin redhead, ten years old today. Maybe Mother ought to cut his hair before the party? He should at least wash it.

But first, the milking.

It was his first chore every morning. The cowhands would have already been up, roped their ponies out of the corral, saddled, breakfasted, and moved on with the ranch work for the day, leaving the barn empty except for the two milk cows. And they'd be making a racket if Tip were late. Between the two of them, Tip would get a whole bucket of milk, enough for breakfast and lunch and for making a quart or so of butter. They'd be ready for another milking in the late afternoon.

Every morning. Every afternoon. Every day. He'd rather be out riding with the hands but, he consoled himself, at least it was summer. Milking the cows in the winter was far worse.

———

"That's a good boy," his mother said as he poured the bucket of milk through a towel stretched across the opening of a large brown crock. "It's a special day! You're already ten years old! I expect that by next year, you'll be up with the hands and herding cows like a grown-up. But for this morning, I'm making pancakes special for you and Lucy."

Oh, no, Tip thought: Pancakes. Either the lumps would be the size of his thumbnail or the batter so thin that they broke into pieces when flipped in the pan. He preferred eggs because you couldn't ruin eggs. He'd make sure plenty of butter and honey was on the table.

Lucy, as usual, was chattering away. Four years younger than Tip, her daily chores were few and would be done with Mother.

"Your father's working in his study this morning, so you two keep everything quiet," his mother said, waving a spoon dripping with batter and shushing Lucy. "Tipton, move the milk cows up to new grass. They need to fatten up before fall comes. Let's all get our chores done this morning. This afternoon, I'll make the best birthday cake you've ever tasted, and we'll get the house ready for the party."

————

Having slathered his pancakes in honey and drunk as much milk as possible, Tip was soon outdoors, flicking the end of a rope against the two rumps waddling ahead of him. The air was still and already getting hot. He breathed deeply as the path swung by the river. The scent of the tall grasses along the bank was always cool and fresh.

He caught a quick movement from the corner of his eye, but before he could turn, a rough hand stuffed a wad of something in his mouth and a bony arm looped a rope around him that held his arms tight against his body. In a flash, two men had him hogtied and shoved into the grass beside the path. His hat had fluttered to the side of the path and now lay upside down in the grass.

He could see them clearly now—two deeply tanned men with painted stripes on their faces, chests, and arms.

They wore no shirts, but had deerskin leggings and breechclouts fringed with tassels.

Comanches!

They ran up on the last milk cow and quickly cut its throat. Before the cow finished jerking, her bag was cut off. The two men held it up to their mouths and gulped whatever milk remained in the udders, the white juice mixing with blood as it ran over their faces.

Hacking deep into the hindquarter of the cow, one man ripped back the hide and cut several strips of meat, alternating putting them in his mouth and throwing them to his partner. No time for a fire meant they'd gobble up as much as they could now and tuck the rest under their belts.

Satisfied, the two young men gave a string of shrill calls and whoops and shot their arrows into the cow and toward the house, grabbed Tip around the waist, and half-dragged him to two horses tied in hiding next to the canyon wall. Sitting him upright behind his partner, the second man tied one of Tip's feet with a leather strip, ran it under the horse, and tied it to his other foot. His hands were similarly bound around the waist of his captor. No jumping off to escape.

The horses leaped up the road, crossed to the riverbed, and a mad race was on.

Tip's hands were soon hurting from the rawhide around his wrists, but his legs hurt worse. His thighs were rubbing hard up against the Indian saddle, fashioned more like a pack saddle than a western saddle, and it was only a couple of hours before the tough fabric of his overalls had torn and the skin was worn through to blood. But falling to the side or slipping back over the rump of the horse filled him with a fear that overwhelmed the pain in his body, and he held on tight.

Kidnapped! He had heard stories of people taken by Indians, and Comanches were said to be the worst.

His fears gave way to panic, then to despair and anguish, his tears running down the back of the man to whom he was tied.

The Comanche men rode for hours, driving their horses relentlessly in and out of canyons, onto mesa tops, and out into the high country foothills. Tip could tell that they changed directions repeatedly. Once, they stopped and set fire to the tall grass around them, riding ahead of the flames as the smoke covered them. The ash and swirling winds wiped away their tracks.

By darkness, they reached a deep ravine far to the north of the ranch. Below, five or six other men squatted next to a string of stolen horses. A horse had been killed and butchered, a fire built, and hunks of meat had been wrapped around sticks. Men were roasting the meat over the flames.

Tip's bonds were cut, and he was thrown to the ground. A few minutes later, the horse's liver was tossed to him. He hungrily stuffed it into his mouth, hardly waiting to chew, and then vomited from the sickening taste of still-warm blood.

It was only minutes before Tip was shoved onto one of the stolen horses, his legs retied around the belly and his hands around the neck. Driving their stolen herd in front, the Comanches kicked their horses and sprinted out of the ravine. Tip's horse was jerked along by a rope.

———

Day after day, night after night, stopping for only a few hours of sleep, the band of raiders raced across the land.

Sometimes they headed toward the sun, sometimes away from it. The land changed from mountains to vast stretches of grassland—flat, with no mesas, no rivers, and no trees.

Miles and miles of tall, dry, yellow grass as far as Tip could see made long, slow waves as the wind blew over it.

Once on the prairie, the hard-riding group took longer breaks to eat and sleep. Tip was viciously hot and hungry and thirsty and tired and sore. Being strapped to the horse had tortured his muscles so that they were almost useless.

His shirt had torn enough under the constant rubbing of his overalls that his neck and shoulders were long burned from the sun. He could feel the heat on his forehead. Without his hat, he correctly guessed that freckles now covered his entire face.

Every so often, the raiding party stopped, dug a shallow hole in the ground, and filled it with small sticks to build a fire. They threw handfuls of grass into the flames to make a thick, black smoke. Using a blanket to cover and then uncover the column of smoke, individual puffs of smoke billowed high into the sky. Soon after, other Indians appeared on the horizon, usually driving small herds of horses and sometimes with other captives—white, brown, black —all children. Within a week, more than a hundred men had joined together and were pushing upward of three hundred horses and mules across the plains.

While they were stopped, Tip talked to the children around him. They were mostly from Texas, some from Oklahoma and New Mexico. As young as seven, as old as fourteen. Two or three spoke only Spanish. Several spoke what he recognized as German, which he did not understand. When any of them talked to the others, it was in frightened whispers.

"Where are you from? How old are you? Anybody coming after you?"

"Don't know, but pretty sure the Army's coming... my family's coming...my father's coming...won't be long, they're right behind us."

But Tip believed they all knew that no one was coming. It had been too fast, too far, too hard. They had all heard the stories.

Nobody ever caught Comanches.

A week later or perhaps two, the sea of grass abruptly halted on the rim of a wide canyon, wider than Tip had ever seen and much deeper than the canyons around the ranch back home. Bound by tall cliffs of sandstone, the rugged canyon appeared suddenly out of the north and broadened like a wide gash through the flat land around it.

A product of eons of erosion cutting through the layers of clay, sand, and rock, the canyon walls were striped with reds, whites, browns, and tans, the different layers of sediment witness to ages past. A stream ran through the bottom.

Tip couldn't believe what he saw—more Indian teepees than he could count were scattered up and down the canyon floor, as far as he could see in both directions.

Hundreds of men, women, and children, old and young, were bustling about. It was more people than he remembered ever seeing in town.

The horse herd was driven in a different direction, and as the remaining riders worked their way down a narrow, dusty trail, the canyon echoed with shouts and yells and whoops.

The riders reached the center of the canyon and began a parade through the camp while everyone, the children especially, greeted them with yells and yodels. Tip's legs were slapped and grabbed and pinched. He tried to kick the hands away, having no sympathy for their pleasure in his capture.

As his pony pulled along at a fast clip, Tip stared at his surroundings. The teepees were painted with symbols in yellow, red, and black. Leather shields with feathers tied in their centers were hung around the entryways. Scattered among the teepees were long bows, hatchets, long guns, quivers of arrows, buffalo robes and blankets, and hides stretched across forms for drying. Everywhere were ropes strung between poles with strips of drying meat.

Smoke from a hundred fires made the scene feel even more hot and dry than it felt already.

The captives were led off in different directions. Tip was roughly pulled from his horse, his coveralls and boots were taken, and he was thrown into the stream, where three women scoured the dirt of almost a month's worth of travel from his skin and hair. The rough hands against his skin were painful, and Tip often howled. His yelps were ignored.

Taken naked from the stream, he was brought directly before the chief of all the Comanches in the canyon. The old man ran his hand through Tip's thick red hair, already dry and frizzy.

That hair was an everlasting gift from his father, Mother used to say. Not a man in a hundred has hair like this, Father used to say. The chief must have liked it because he took Tip in as a member of his family.

Two or three women now herded him away, throwing a set of breeches at him. Then they began swatting him with sticks and forced him to work. He was to gather wood and water, tend the fire, and beat the dust from buffalo blankets. He was slave labor, all his work done under a constant barrage of insults and strikes with a stick. When he was caught falling down, cringing from their sticks, or crying with sorrow or fear, they beat him worse.

———

The next afternoon, in a broad meadow, a ring was created by circling ropes around poles stuck in the ground.

Tip had heard that Comanches ate white children, so he figured it was time for him to be tortured and eaten.

Instead, as drums announced the beginning of a

celebration, he was pushed into the middle of the ring to meet an Indian boy about his size. It was a fight, and the crowd cheered and laughed as Tip was twisted, thrown, punched, kicked, and wrestled while he cried, yelled, and blubbered. Bloodied and dirty, he was dragged from the ring and thrown into the stream to wash himself.

That night, the chief spoke to him. Tip certainly knew none of the Comanche's language and the chief knew no English, but they each knew a little Spanish, so they were able to make themselves understood.

Fighting is not punishment, the chief said. It is training.

Tip was no longer white—that was past. Tip was now Comanche, and he would serve the chief.

He was no longer a captive. He was a son.

CHAPTER 2

BLUFF, UTAH, PRESENT DAY

Mogi Franklin carefully shifted his new light-gray, 2X beaver cowboy hat so that it sat just barely above his ears, perfectly straight across his forehead, and just the right distance above his eyebrows to not interfere with a good squint.

Satisfied with his appearance in the mirror, he slowly lowered his hands toward an imaginary two-pistol gun belt around his waist and stood tall as he faced the image of what had now become a villainous outlaw.

He pushed his toes into the fronts of his brand-new cowboy boots, spread his feet a couple of inches more, and went into a semi-crouch as he braced for whipping out his imaginary pistols to bring the wrath of justice down on the head of the evil man before him.

He spat an imaginary stream of tobacco-stained saliva into the imaginary dust of the imaginary street beneath his feet. "You want me, you rotten bag of dog vomit?" he said in a gravelly voice. "Then prepare to die!"

He saw an imperceptibly small change in the outlaw's eyes. Mogi's hands moved like lightning, jerking the pistols from their holsters and cocking the hammers as he leveled the barrels at the outlaw's chest. The guns roared as they belched hot lead across the room, ripping through the outlaw's flesh and spraying blood all over the wall.

"What in the world are you doing?"

Jennifer Franklin stood in the doorway of Mogi's bedroom with a quizzical look on her face. She was seventeen, three years older than her brother, and a half-foot shorter. With thick, brown hair cut short, she was strong, athletic, and physically graceful.

Deftly blowing the smoke from each barrel, twirling the guns in unison as he slid them smoothly back into their holsters, Sheriff Mogi straightened from his crouch, took off his hat, and slid it over his heart as he turned to face his sister with his humblest expression.

"I'm sorry, Ma'am, if I've insulted your tender sensibilities by killing this miserable piece of humanity, but justice has been served today, and now this brave, new country is ready for fine women like yourself to raise children in a land of peace and honor and God-fearing people."

Jennifer rolled her eyes. Being a people person and

a keen observer of human nature, it made being around her brother pretty interesting at times. "I think I'll ask Mom if therapy would help, but until then, you might consider that most gunfighters would probably, at least, have put on pants before a gunfight."

Mogi looked down and blushed as he realized that his cowboy hat and boots were set off only by his tighty-whities.

"Uh..."

Jennifer continued down the hall, sat down at the dining table, and began to thumb through a magazine. It was the end of May, and only two more days of school meant the coming freedom from the daily grind of education.

Mogi reappeared in the boots and hat, but this time also in a T-shirt and jeans. He moved to Jennifer's side and unfolded a large New Mexico state highway map across the table.

"Okay, so maybe I won't exactly rid the country of outlaws, but have you seen where I'm going? I never knew Granddad had friends like this. Look!" He picked up a pencil and circled a small area on the map east of Las Vegas, New Mexico, north of Interstate 40 as it passed between the towns of Santa Rosa and Tucumcari.

"This is where the Buffalo Skull Ranch is. I looked it up on the web. There's a half-million acres. It's a big ranching operation with a lot of cattle, but part of it is a dude ranch with an old hacienda that's been converted to a hotel. They provide horseback rides, hikes, jeep tours, a swimming pool, tennis courts, cowboy cookouts, and all sorts of stuff. Lots of famous people and movie stars have stayed there. I don't know exactly what I'll be doing, but I'll be a ranch hand, helping out with the cattle. I hope they don't expect me to wrestle steers or anything."

"You realize, of course," Jennifer replied, "that you'll actually be expected to work?"

Mogi acted surprised. "Hey, I can work! I'm big for my age. I can keep up with anybody. It's about time I started making myself into a real man."

"Oh, good grief," his sister moaned.

Mogi was fourteen and tall for his age, but his muscles had not yet caught up with his bones, so he was gangly and spindly and a little awkward, which is to say, normal for his position in life. He took after his mom's side of the family in his looks and his shyness, but seemed to be the sum of both families on the brain side. He was way smarter than his friends, quick-minded, mentally disciplined and orderly, and had a natural talent for solving puzzles.

"And not only do I expect to get good at cowboyin', but I'll become part of the heritage of all cowboyhood."

"What are you talking about?"

"I've been reading up on the greatest cowboy of all time—Colonel Charlie Goodnight. Look at the map."

He used his hand to smooth the map down to the southeastern New Mexico border.

"Charlie Goodnight became the most famous cattle-man in Texas. He was a Texas Ranger during the Civil War, and after that, he blazed a cattle trail from Texas to Wyoming by taking herds of cattle over to the Pecos River in New Mexico and then following it north.

"After becoming the biggest rancher in Colorado, Goodnight moved to Texas and started one of the largest cattle ranches in the world around Palo Duro Canyon. He became one of the most influential people in Texas history."

"But what's important is this."

He drew a line on the map from Fort Sumner north through his circle around the Buffalo Skull Ranch and up to the New Mexican border by Raton.

"When he took his cattle up the Pecos, he turned at Santa Rosa and drove his herd right through the land that became the Buffalo Skull Ranch. I'll be riding the range right on top of where thousands of Texas Long-horns grazed. Cowboys, Indians, Texas Longhorns, cattle drives, Indian battles, buffalo herds, the Santa Fe Trail, the Civil War, the war with Mexico—all that history happened right where I'm going to be.

"Granddad said I'll be learning to rope and ride, and herd cattle, and shoot at coyotes, and sleep out under the stars, and be livin' the cowboy life."

Mogi began jumping around the living room, drawing his pistols and shooting bad guys, swinging his rope, spurring his horse, and attacking the sofa as he wrestled a steer to the ground.

Jennifer shook her head in disbelief. "I hope Granddad doesn't regret offering you up as summer help for this place," she said. "He and the ranch manager went to college together, and you working there for the summer was meant as something that would benefit you both.

"Having a crazy fourteen-year-old may be more than they bargained for."

————

TWO MONTHS LATER

Jennifer and her grandfather had left Bluff, Utah— Jennifer and Mogi's hometown—early that morning and driven across Northern New Mexico, down the Española Valley, through Santa Fe, and an hour east to Las Vegas.

"Are you worried?" Granddad asked.

"I'm not sure," Jennifer replied. "Mogi's never seemed this anxious before. He only calls when he goes to town because they don't have cell service on the ranch. He called pretty often in June, but I stopped hearing from him until last week. He sounded scared, which is really not like him at all. He was avoiding telling me something, I'm sure, or maybe trying to not be overheard."

"I can believe that there's no cell phone service out there," Granddad said. "The ranch is close to some of the last land in New Mexico to be settled and is a good forty miles from any city. If he'd had to use the ranch phone or a phone on a trip to town, there would likely have been people around. That might be reason enough for him to be cautious, if he wanted to talk to you about a private matter or something.

"I hate to think that I put him into ranch work before he was ready for it. I figured fourteen was pretty young, but Bud had his kids on the ranch since they were born, and they all did fine. Bud said that he'd go gentle on the boy. He said there were always low-level jobs to do, but you know how intense your brother can get."

Jennifer looked directly at Granddad.

"Is it true that a lot of the cattle have died?" she asked. "I mean, they were murdered or something? Mogi talked about mysterious circumstances and the cowboys being scared out of their wits. He even mentioned rumors about aliens from another planet, but that's kind of a New Mexico thing. He doesn't know what's happening, but some people are worried that the water has turned bad."

"I talked with Bud last night," Granddad replied, "and I'm afraid the news is not good. About the first of July, several steers were found stone-cold dead in a side canyon of the Canadian River, which runs right through the ranch. There were no marks on them, no signs of accident or predators. They looked in good health and weren't injured. Every few days after that, more dead cattle started turning up in various places along the river. The state sent doctors from their science labs to investigate, but everybody is baffled. They don't know what's wrong.

"This is a serious situation for a cattle ranch. You remember how bad the Mad Cow disease was in England, where they had to destroy thousands of animals to keep the disease from spreading? This is the same situation. If a definite cause can't be determined, the drastic step is to assume that it's the cows themselves that have the disease, and Bud would have to put down every one of several thousand cattle. He wouldn't be able to sell the meat or anything, which means that the herd would be a total loss, and that's a whole lot of money. I doubt the ranch could ever recover. The owners of the ranch would have to sell the ranch for pennies on the dollar, and Bud would be out on the street."

The trip through the middle of New Mexico had taken them through mountain valleys where the deep greens of forests contrasted with the pale yellows of semi-desert foothills. East of Las Vegas, they left the mountains behind and crossed into a broad expanse of grass.

Suddenly, they dropped over a ridge and found themselves descending a long, sloping highway that cut across the face of a high cliff. As the pickup curved slowly down the narrow road, Jennifer watched the strong winds battering the trees as the heat of the cliff face channeled hot winds upward. Several ravens darted in and out of the wind currents as they played along the rocks.

"What else did your brother have to say?" Granddad asked.

"He didn't say much about what he's been doing, just that his back hurts and he's hungry all the time. He must be growing again. At Christmas, he had a growth spurt, and we did all we could to pull him out of the refrigerator every day. I think he grew an inch just in December. He's been taller than me for a long time, but I'm not sure I'm ready for a brother who's a giant."

"You don't mind working at the ranch for two weeks, do you?" Granddad asked. "It seemed like the best way to get someone inside the operations of the ranch to look for anything out of the ordinary. I'm usually not so secretive, but Bud is under a lot of pressure, and I'd like to help him out."

"Oh, no, that's fine. It'll give me some spending money. I'm not sure what I'm supposed to do, though."

"Just hang around and watch. You're a pretty sharp kid, you and your brother both. You've got a gift for understanding people. I figure if there's anything out of place, you'll see it. Speaking of that, did your brother say anything about the people?"

"Nope. He said that he'd tell us more when we came. He said you'd especially be interested in what he's found out."

"That sounds mysterious enough. Did he explain?"

"As a matter of fact," Jennifer said with a grin, "he said he's been getting mixed up with a few good guys and a few bad guys of history, Spanish land grants, and children kidnapped by the Comanches."

"That's my boy!" Granddad said with a laugh. Anything connected to the history of the American Southwest was especially delightful to Mogi and Jennifer's grandfather.

"Anything else?"

"Well," Jennifer said, "I'm not sure he was serious, but he said he saw a ghost."

CHAPTER 3

D riving Highway 419, Jennifer and Granddad crossed the Canadian River just before a sign pointed the right turn to Buffalo Skull Ranch Headquarters. Thirty minutes later, after passing a dirt airstrip and some hangars, they pulled into a group of buildings and corrals nestled against the bottom of an isolated mesa.

There was no doubt it was a working ranch, with corrals made out of thick pipe fencing, large, open-sided shelters that held a few hundred rolls of hay, and several trucks, horse trailers, tractors, and other machinery lined up in various places around several large metal buildings.

Two hundred yards away, tall, spreading cotton-woods surrounded a massive adobe house with curved arches that sheltered a porch and a large courtyard.

"This is a big place," Jennifer said as she stepped

out of the pickup, stretched, and looked around the horizon.

"Hey, isn't that the famous ol' Ben Franklin that I see?" came a loud voice from a man stepping out of the headquarters building.

"Well, probably not the one you're thinking of, but I can do in a pinch!" Granddad responded with a laugh, grabbing the man's outstretched hand and vigorously shaking it. "How are you doing, Bud?"

"Well, things have been better, but we'll get to that later," the man said. "And this must be our newest employee. Mighty pleased to have you, young lady," he said, cheerfully shaking Jennifer's hand.

"Where's that grandson of mine?" Granddad asked. "Has he worked out for you?"

"Well, it's about time for the boys to be in. Let's go see if he's back."

Bud had broad shoulders to go with a stocky torso and a considerable belly hanging over his belt. He had the bow-legged gait of a man who had spent a lot of time on a horse. As they walked, Bud talked.

"That's some grandkid you got there. He was pretty shy to begin with, and all skinny arms and legs, but we just threw him in with everybody else. We kept him on a horse as much as we could for the first couple of days to break him in quick. I swear it was the funniest thing I ever saw when he crawled off his horse at the end of the first day. He certainly doesn't have much padding in his backside, that's for sure.

"After that, we had him workin' on a horse a half-day, then workin' in the barn and on the hay truck. I thought that maybe he'd be more comfortable workin' around the headquarters, but he warmed up pretty good for a green-horn and was asking for more. After a week or so, we let him go with the brandin' crew, helpin' with the horses and the chuckwagon.

"And, by golly, after the first month, he was gettin' the hang of it—ropin' calves, ridin' drag when we moved a herd, and workin' the remuda in the mornin'—that's the string of horses we keep for the cowhands to ride. He got good enough that the various camp bosses wanted him on their crews.

"That boy's a quick learner. He pays attention, and he listens, and he's got a memory to beat the band. I put him countin' cows one day when we were brandin', and he not only kept up with the total, but he remembered every single ear tag of almost two hundred critters. Not that we needed the information, since we had it written down, but he did amaze the old hands, for sure. I wish I had a few more like that."

They reached a barn area with several corrals and gates.

In the distance, Jennifer saw a group of riders loping across a pasture to the east, raising a small cloud of dust.

"This is a group comin' in from Camp Three. The range is divided into six camps, each about twenty to thirty thousand acres. Each camp has a range boss, a wrangler, a helper, and five or six cowhands. They each manage about fifteen hundred head of cattle. We move 'em to grass, then to water a couple times a day.

"When we do the brandin', like we did in June, we pull hands from all of the camps and form up an old-time brandin' outfit, complete with a chuckwagon and beddin' wagon. The crew moves from one camp to another, herdin' up, cuttin' out the calves, and puttin' a good brand on 'em.

"They also get their shots and we take samples of blood for DNA records, then tag 'em on the ears with a unique ID. Each ranch hand has a bedroll and sleeps out with the wagons at night. We cheat a little bit by bringin' in fresh water every day and providin' portable toilets, but what can you say? It's still a good bit of tradition to go with the hard work.

"Your grandson seemed to like it all. And, by the way, if you don't take that boy home pretty soon, I'm going to start chargin' for his meals. He's almost made raisin' beef unprofitable."

The riders slowed their horses to a trot, came through a gate, and then walked the horses to a corral. One leaned over and opened a gate that led to the side of the barn and allowed six of the riders to pass through. The seventh kept the horse to a walk as he neared the three observers.

The seventh rider brought his horse to a halt, smoothly swung his right leg over the back of the saddle, and stepped to the ground. He slid the reins over the horse's head and quickly tied them to the top rail of the corral fence. Ducking under the reins, he walked toward Jennifer.

The man was tall and tanned and walked confidently as he removed his gloves and tucked them under his belt.

A fine dust covered his light-blue collarless shirt, fitted over a pair of worn jeans. He wore a large buckle on a wide leather belt, and a sweat-stained yellow bandanna was tied around his neck.

The man reached up and removed his broad-brimmed, tall-crowned straw hat, which he started swishing against himself, sending a few puffs of dust around him.

But it really wasn't until he smiled that Jennifer saw that this man was her brother.

"Oh, my!" was all she could say before he gave her a hug.

"Hey, my long-lost sister has come to visit the Old West!" he said out loud. But in a smaller voice, directly into her ear, he said, "You don't know how glad I am you're here."

Granddad shook his hand. Mogi wasn't yet quite as tall as the old man.

"Oh, wow, a real cowboy. Please sir, can I have an autograph?"

Mogi laughed as he grabbed the man for a hug. After that, he shook Bud's hand.

"I've got to get my horse unsaddled, combed down, and fed," Mogi said. "How about Jennifer comes with me and we'll catch up to you later?"

"Well," Bud said, "I'll give her a little time off, but this lady is a new staff member, and we don't just let staff go around loafin'. Y'all take your time, but we've got a chuckwagon dinner tonight, so clean up and get ready to work."

Mogi smiled, untied the horse, and led him through the gate, talking softly to him as Jennifer walked alongside.

Through the barn's side door, he led the horse to a stall next to the tack room. He took a short rope, slung a loop over the horse's head, and tied it to a rail. He peeled the bridle over the horse's ears, removed the bit, and then hung it from a peg.

He hung the stirrups on the saddle horn, undid the long belt of leather holding the cinch, and finally slid the well-worn saddle off the horse's back and carried it to a rack inside the tack room. Pulling off the thick saddle blanket, he gave it a good whap against the stall and draped it over a hanging rod, making sure to fluff it out for a good airing.

Retrieving two stiff brushes, he handed one to Jennifer and they started working out the areas of sweat on the horse's back.

"This is the hardest work I've ever done," Mogi said, "and I still don't like getting up at four thirty in the morning to work an hour before I eat breakfast. I've always made fun of the Hollywood cowboys in the movies, but this stuff is really hard.

"You wouldn't believe how smart and resourceful these people are. I've never met such talented people when it comes to making fast decisions. When you're out in the pastures, you don't have a chance to call in to headquarters and ask for help. When you see a sick cow, you take care of it. When you see a fence down, you take care of it. If a cow is stuck in the mud, you figure out how you get it out. Whether it's cowgirl or cowboy, these people know what they're doing, and they fulfill the responsibilities they've been given. I like it here, even if I do have to get up early."

"How'd you get so tall? You weren't this tall when you left."

Mogi laughed. "Well, don't be fooled—a lot of it is boots and hat. I've got almost two-inch heels on these things, and my hat has six inches of crown. However, I do think I've grown a bit since I got here. I don't mind the height, but my back hurts all the time, and I'm *always* hungry."

He circled the horse and glanced around, making sure no one else was within hearing distance.

"They found another group of dead cattle last night," he said, lowering his voice. "That makes over a hundred dead in only five or six weeks. The state inspector came out this morning. I think they're about to close down the ranch. You can't tell, but Bud is worried sick. Has he talked to you and Granddad yet?"

"No," Jennifer said quietly. "He put us off until after dinner tonight."

"What are you supposed to do while you're here?"

"This was Granddad's idea. Bud's hired me as a worker in the hacienda, but I'm supposed to be watching for anybody who might hold a grudge or complaint against the ranch. Bud is worried some-body's working from inside the ranch to cause these deaths. He can't believe the water's gone bad after all these years, and nothing else has changed. That means that somebody is killing the cattle, but he doesn't know how or why."

Mogi nodded. "Well, just having you here is good news. Since I've been working around the different camps all summer, Bud's put me riding fence for the next two weeks until it's time to go home. That will allow me to go anywhere on the ranch without looking out of place. I'm supposed to check the countryside for anything unusual.

"It would help if we knew what we were looking for, but nobody's got a clue. The state investigators are stumped, but without a clear cause for the deaths, they have to assume it's a disease, which is really bad news, so I'm hoping we'll discover a new breed of poisonous snake that's been biting the cows, or maybe a mad scientist who's killing them with sound waves or something."

"Do you help out at the hacienda? Do you know the people who work there?" Jennifer asked.

"I haven't worked with the house staff or the ranch guests at all, except for meeting people at the chuckwagon suppers. The hacienda's off limits to the ranch hands. There aren't that many guest rooms and suites, maybe eighteen or twenty, so I imagine there are forty to fifty people max at any one time. The tour guides and wranglers who work with them are typically men and women who have been here a long time. They take the guests out, teach them to ride, take them up some of the canyons to the streams and waterfalls, and ride out to the camps to show them how the ranch works. Things like that.

"The guests get their meals like they would at a bed-and-breakfast, unless it's Saturday night, like tonight, when there's a family chuckwagon meal out on the patio. It's also different on Sunday mornings, when they have a brunch instead of a separate breakfast and lunch. At the chuckwagon meal, everybody at the ranch comes together for a really big feed, and a cowboy band provides entertainment. I hate to say it, but I'm beginning to like country music."

"So what's this about seeing a ghost?"

Mogi looked quickly from side to side. "We'll talk about that later. The ranch hands are a superstitious bunch, and as spooked as they are about the cows, any serious talk about ghosts makes everything worse. Besides, I want Granddad around when I tell you."

Finished with the brushing, Mogi picked the hair out of the brushes and returned them to the tack room. He untied the halter and led the horse out to a small corral behind the barn. Letting the horse go as he slid the loop off, he went back to the barn and returned with a bucket of grain. He dumped the bucket into a trough near the gate, and the horse began to hungrily munch the oats.

"I'll let you go on over to the hacienda. I've got to get cleaned up over at the bunkhouse so I'll be presentable for the general public." He gave Jennifer a hug and took off at a trot toward another outbuilding.

"Hey," Jennifer called after him.

Mogi turned around.

"What happened to your other hat—the gray one?"

Mogi laughed. "It blew off on the second day I was here, and one of the cows chewed a chunk out of it. The other guys were making fun of it anyway. I had bought a dress hat, so they took me to town and bought me one made for working."

CHAPTER 4

J ennifer walked to the hacienda's kitchen and introduced herself. She was heartily welcomed and immediately assigned to preparing the drinks—lemonade, tea, and water—and setting out stacks of plates, glasses, utensils, and napkins.

Pork ribs, sausage, and chicken were cooking outside on a large barbeque grill, while large beef roasts were cooking in a chuckwagon fire pit on the side of the patio area. Inside, the kitchen staff prepared salad, coleslaw, potato salad, various meat sauces, and a dozen loaves of bread.

In the kitchen of the headquarters building, where the ranch hands and staff usually ate, an array of desserts were being prepared—two chocolate sheet cakes with chocolate icing, one pan each of peach and cherry cobbler, a large bowl of banana pudding, and several plates of cookies.

Having put on his best clothes, which looked just like his other clothes minus the dirt and dust, Mogi arrived and helped with the roasts. That morning, the chuckwagon cook had dug a long trench and spread an old canvas tarp along the inside. After wrapping layers of muslin around several pieces of beef, each about the size of a small turkey, he placed the roasts in a line from one end of the trench to the other and then folded over the sides and ends of the tarp, tucking the sides in as he went. Several inches of dirt were then pushed over the tarp, and a long, narrow fire was built over the buried roasts, creating an authentic cattle-drive oven.

As suppertime drew close, a smaller fire was started between two tall iron stakes that had been driven into the ground. A metal rod set across the stakes held several coffee pots a few inches above the flames. Two large, cast-iron Dutch ovens full of beans sat directly on the coals.

When Mogi arrived, the cook carefully pushed the coals to one side, raked the dirt away, and peeled back the tarp.

He transferred two of the roasts to a cutting board where the muslin was removed, the meat sliced, and huge platters filled. More roasts would be moved to the boards as needed.

"You put on a pretty good feed, Bud," Granddad said to his friend as they sat in chairs under a canopy of broad-leafed cottonwood trees.

"Well, we try. The proof of success in the dude ranch business is repeat customers. And seein' the chuckwagon with the cook and all the cowboys is one of the things people come back for. It's a lot of fun for us, too. The cowhands and other staff like to visit with the guests, and everybody really enjoys the band. There're lots of cowboy tales told, true and maybe not so true, but everybody has a good time. The cowgirls get a lot of the questions, with people wantin' to know what it's like for women to work with cattle, how they put up with riding all day, and what it's like to work with a bunch of dirty old cowboys. People are surprised—some of the women are more skilled than the men. It all depends on how much you love this life."

Mogi helped Jennifer spread tablecloths on the tables and bring large jars of drinks from the kitchen to the drink table. The guests were already milling around the huge flagstone patio, watching the cook prepare the food, talking with the cowboys and the other guests, and watching the sun set in a rose-colored sky over the distant mountains. Several children played around the tables.

The banging of a rod against an iron triangle broke through the buzz of conversation, and people started to move toward the buffet-style serving tables. It wasn't long before seventy or more plates were stacked high with meat and salads and beans and bread and anything else people could pile on top without the whole stack sliding off onto their shirt cuffs.

A full assault on the dessert table followed soon after.

A five-member cowboy band began performing with the ringing of the dinner bell, providing an impressive line-up of songs and stories as everyone ate. For almost an hour, the crowd broke into wild applause for the band's songs, tales, and humor.

Mogi and Jennifer worked through the evening, replenishing the food platters and drink jars, serving guests, keeping the area tidy, and then, when the lines in front of the food tables finally disappeared, moving uneaten food back into the kitchen. Then they helped to separate, wrap, mark, and distribute packages to various refrigerators and freezers. The food would be used throughout the week for lunches and dinners.

With several other staff members, the mounds of dirty serving plates, trays, pans, jars, pots, skillets, carving knives, ladles, and tongs were moved to the large sinks and commercial dishwashers. With as many workers as there were, it still took a good hour to get everything washed, dried, and put away.

After the band wrapped up their entertainment, the guests went back to their rooms in the hacienda, the cowboys drifted back to their bunkhouses, and the kitchen staff went to their beds anticipating the Sunday brunch coming in a few short hours.

The patio was now draped in moonlight and silence.

In chairs drawn up to the dying coals of the chuckwagon fire, Mogi, Jennifer, Granddad, and Bud sat in quiet comfort. Bud added a couple more logs to the fire.

"So, what do you think of cowboyin'?" Granddad asked Mogi.

"It's hard work," Mogi replied. "And awfully long

days. I've never done anything like it. I think I've earned a place with the cowboys, but I certainly don't know all that much. The guys I work with are amazing. They know everything about the land and the cattle and the horses, when to do things, what the weather's going to be like and how to adjust for it, when a cow is going to calve, what condition the grass is in, when and where to move a herd. It's pretty awesome."

"Well, if you're tuned up to experience the life of cowboys, then these next two weeks are goin' to be special," Bud said. "We've got about forty people comin' who are associated with the Museum of the American Cowboy in Oklahoma City. In two years, the museum is goin' to celebrate the years of the cattle drives—somewheres between 1850 and 1885, I believe—and the museum staff is comin' out to hold a plannin' retreat.

"The first week is a conference where research people sit around and talk about their areas of expertise and identify what needs to be included in the celebration. The second week is for the museum staff to plan the activities they'll host during the exhibition. I expect there'll be a truckload of stories about cowboys and the West."

Bud leaned back in his chair and carefully looked around the patio. Seeing no one, he leaned forward and put his elbows on his knees, his face changing from a friendly ranch manager into a man with worries. "That is, if there's any ranch left by next week," he said.

He looked at Granddad. "Ben, you've got to help me—I'm dyin' here!"

Another hour passed as Bud and their Granddad spoke and Mogi and Jennifer listened. Bud reviewed the happenings from the past month—what he had seen, what he thought about the cattle, the locations of the deaths, the State Science Lab investigation and reports, and the rumors going around about who, what, and why.

"Bud," Granddad said finally, "I don't know what we can do, but we'll do all we can. I'm going to poke around Las Vegas and Santa Fe and see what I can learn. I'm leaving you with a young woman who has a gift for understanding people and a young man who has a gift for solving mysteries. Right now, I'd like to see an overall map of the ranch and the surrounding country before I turn in."

With that, Bud and their grandfather got up, carried their chairs to the small patio tables that had already been set out for the morning, and headed to the headquarters building.

Mogi laid another log on the fire.

"Okay, I can't wait any longer," Jennifer said. "Tell me about the ghost."

CHAPTER 5

"It's a long story," Mogi said to Jennifer. "It starts a long time ago, so stay with me.

"Around the 1850s, a man named Martin Mulvaney was a lawyer in St. Louis. He was a big man—a very big man, way over six feet tall, probably three hundred pounds—and he had flaming red hair. His wife was a thin, delicate thing from one of the richest St. Louis families.

"Mr. Mulvaney had a nose for money, so he up and moved his family to Denver, chasing the growing waves of railroad and mining interests in the West. After a few years, he partnered up with a lawyer named Terence Hetley. They set their sights on becoming rich, so they started working on the issues surrounding Spanish and Mexican land grants. In 1861, they moved to Las Vegas, New Mexico, and set up a law office.

"Original land grants were pieces of land given to individuals in return for their service to the Spanish crown. The king gave tracts of land to conquistadors, missionaries, and settlers, for example. After Mexico won its independence from Spain in the early 1800s, Mexico also gave tracts of land to its worthy citizens. Then the United States defeated Mexico and created the New Mexico territory, which included Arizona. The United States, however, didn't automatically understand or recognize land grants, so people bought and sold land on American rules.

"By the mid-1850s, it was a real mess. Land ownership was fought over constantly. Back then, most of the arguments ended up in the US court system, and that's where corrupt lawyers swindled people.

"Martin Mulvaney and Terrence Hetley were both corrupt lawyers. They took on land disputes by representing poor landowners, but instead of charging money for their services, which the landowners didn't have, they took part of the land as payment. The longer the dispute, the more they charged, and the more land they got in payment.

"Since most of their clients spoke little or no English, the two lawyers cheated landowners almost at will. By the time the Civil War was over, the two of them owned about a million acres, scattered around the central and northeastern parts of the state, for which they hadn't paid a dime.

"Okay. Now the cattle drives and railroads come into play. Remember Charlie Goodnight, the famous cowboy I was telling you about? Well, Goodnight made the first big cattle drive from southern New

Mexico to Colorado in 1866, crossing some of the land that Mulvaney and Hetley owned. Meanwhile, the railroads were talking about building rail lines from Colorado down to Las Vegas and Santa Fe, which also went across the land the lawyers owned.

"Given the situation, Martin Mulvaney decided on a master plan—he sold all the land he owned to his partner in exchange for one huge piece of grassland outside of Las Vegas. It was like a hundred thousand acres. Then, once the railroad was built, Mulvaney planned to build a huge complex of corrals, holding pens, and loading ramps. Then he'd advertise the land as an endpoint for anybody making cattle drives up that side of New Mexico.

"It was a pretty good plan and, if it had worked, the Las Vegas area would have grown into a major shipping depot just like Abilene, Texas, and Dodge City, Kansas. Martin Mulvaney would have been rich beyond his wildest dreams.

"Expecting that he was going to be fabulously rich, Mulvaney decided to build a house—a really big house appropriate for a rich man."

"He let his sweet little wife, along with their two children, a boy and a girl, pick a beautiful piece of land in a deep canyon as the spot to build the house, right where a side river joins the Canadian River. There was lots of water, beautiful sandstone cliffs, tall cottonwood trees, natural protection from the wind, lots of stone to build with, and it was already on land that Mulvaney owned.

"So Mr. Mulvaney had a house built, and we're

talking a *big* house. It had two full stories with a reception hall, a kitchen, a huge dining room that could be used as a dance floor, a billiard room, and a library, all on the first floor. There were five or six bedrooms on the second floor and then a couple of attic rooms under a massive sloped roof. A two-story porch wrapped all around the house, just like the plantation mansions in the South, with two stairways.

"In the middle of the house, Mulvaney built a huge chimney, maybe twelve feet square and twenty feet tall. Every major room in the house had some part of the chimney in it, so every major room could have a fireplace or a wood-burning stove, and all the piping could be run together up this stone chimney.

"When it was time for the outside walls and the roof to be built, he brought out a dozen stonemasons from St. Louis and had the whole outside of the house covered in stone. He even ordered slate tile from back east and had it put on the roof.

"It was a fortress when it was finished. It was far beyond anything else around the country, so people called it *Mulvaney Castle*. In 1869, Martin Mulvaney moved his family into the house and began what he expected to be the grand life of a cattle baron.

"But things went wrong.

"First, things were heating up for cattle barons in New Mexico. The state legislature was corrupt, and some of the politicians were jealous of the big cattle ranches in eastern New Mexico, especially along the Pecos River. They started putting more taxes on the ranchers.

"Second, Charlie Goodnight, who had been buying cattle from the Pecos River ranches to take up the trail to Colorado, hated taxes even more than politicians, so he changed his cattle drive route, moving it eastward to avoid the Las Vegas area completely. That meant the cattle drives now bypassed Mulvaney's land.

"Third, Mulvaney's partner, Terrence Hetley, was playing under the table, not only cheating his clients but cheating his partner as well. He bought the land on the west side of Mulvaney's land and made an even sweeter deal with the railroad so that the new train route went through his land and not Mulvaney's. So first, Mulvaney misses out on the cattle, and then he misses out on the railroad.

"Then it turns out that the big house Mulvaney built was smack dab in the middle of one of the best Comanche hiding places. The Comanches were the fiercest, wildest Indians of the time. They stole horses, mules, cattle, and children from all over Texas, Oklahoma, Kansas, Nebraska, and even down into Mexico. They'd been using the Canadian River canyons for years as hideouts.

"So everything was going bad for Mr. Mulvaney and his family. But the final blow came in 1870 when Tipton, his ten-year-old son, was kidnapped by the Comanches. The boy's out one morning walking some milk cows to a pasture and—poof!—he's taken.

"Not only is Martin Mulvaney devastated, but his wife goes mostly insane.

"Given everything bad that's happening, he makes

a decision. He sends Lucy, his six-year-old daughter, back to live with relatives in St. Louis, he leaves his wife to be looked after by the cowhands, and he goes into town to see his old partner. Mulvaney's plan is to sell everything he has and go back to St. Louis to start over.

"To do this, he needs Hetley to buy his house and property. Well, not only does Hetley not want to buy the house and property, but he pretty much laughs in Mulvaney's face. Mulvaney actually gets down on his knees and begs, which must have been a terrible and humiliating sight, remembering how big a guy he was. Hetley laughs at him and throws him out into the street.

"Well, something snaps, and Mulvaney explodes, which I guess is something he did a lot. He gets up, turns around, goes back into the office, and beats the stuffing out of Hetley, as well as the hired thug who rushes in to protect his boss. And then, unfortunately, he kills Hetley by breaking his neck. Mulvaney is immediately arrested, taken down to the jail, and is hanging from a rope by morning.

"Some of Mulvaney's friends take the body back to the *castle* and, as you might expect, Mulvaney's wife goes all the way nuts. They bury his body behind the house and everybody leaves except two maids, who are left to care for Mrs. Mulvaney until arrangements can be made to get her back east to her family.

"Two days later, the wife disappears. Even though the maids swear she never left the house, everybody thinks the wife went down to the river and drowned herself. Her body is never found, everybody leaves, and the house is abandoned. Almost immediately, the ghost stories start.

"The house is so far from the city and other ranches that no one goes there. Every now and then, though, a trapper passing through Las Vegas reports seeing a woman dancing on the porch of the old Mulvaney place, usually by the light of a full moon. An Indian reports seeing a woman all dressed in white dancing up on the mesas. Someone else tells of howls and screams and moans echoing off the canyon walls.

"The frontier is a pretty superstitious place, and the Indians, the Hispanics, and the Comanches in particular, never doubted any of these stories. When they believe spirits have taken over a place, they won't go within miles of it. The wife's suicide makes it worse because the whole place is then considered to be cursed by God."

Mogi used his boot to nudge the ends of the logs into the fire.

"And now, finally, I get to my ghost."

CHAPTER 6

"All ranch hands get some time off," Mogi began. "The ranch, of course, has work going on seven days a week, but Bud makes a rotation schedule so we end up with a day or two off each week. Two weeks ago, I had been working the cattle in Camp Six. Camp Six is the northwest part of the ranch that includes where the Canadian River comes out of the cliffs. You and Granddad drove through part of it to get to the ranch gate.

"Hector Valdez is the range boss for Camp Six. He showed me a topographic map to get me familiar with the country, and I noticed the symbol for a house where the Mora and Canadian rivers run together, north of the highway. It's actually labeled *Mulvaney Castle*, believe it or not.

"I asked Hector what the name meant, and that's when he told me the story of Martin Mulvaney. The vehicle road to the house comes from Las Vegas, so you have to, from here, go all the way to Las Vegas and then drive back east if you want to drive to the house. But there's a horse trail on this side of the cliffs, starting right at the highway where it crosses the Canadian, that leads to the canyon.

"Well, you know me. Saturday was my day off, so I saddled a horse and rode out to find the house. It wasn't two hours before I'd left the ranch boundary and gone into the canyon that I was surrounded by thousand-foot cliffs. Right before you get there, the river makes a big *S* curve and then comes out to where the house is located.

"You have to see it to believe it. The house is huge. The porch supports had been made out of stone, so most of those are still standing, but the floors and roof of the wrap-around porch have collapsed all around the building. Most of the walls of the house are still standing because they're held up by all the stonework, but the roof has sagged in a couple of places. There are big piles of tumbleweeds and heaps of old wood and stone, and grass has grown over everything. Sand dunes have even blown up against the foundation. All together, it looks like a big, sad, falling-down house.

"I propped a board up against the foundation to get in through the doorway. There're no doors or windows anymore, so I was able to walk through the whole house.

"The first thing I saw was the chimney—it's right in the center of everything. The doorways are built so you can walk around it, passing through the living room, the kitchen, and two more big rooms, probably the parlor and library. In each room, you can see some stovepipe or fireplace built into the chimney. Even the kitchen stove had its pipe plugged into the chimney. And wherever there was space on the chimney wall not occupied by a fireplace or stovepipes, Mulvaney put in fancy built-in wooden bookcases.

"A stairway was still intact enough to walk up, so I went upstairs. Each bedroom is pretty big, with a window on the outside wall and a door that opened to the porch. There's still quite a lot of wallpaper on the walls. Once again, each room has a fireplace or stovepipe opening in the chimney, which I think was a really smart thing to do.

"Next to the chimney in one of the rooms was a closet that had a narrow stairway leading up to the attic. The attic has two small rooms under the long sides of the roof, with a small hallway that joins them and dormers that project out through the roof.

"Back outside, I spent an hour or so looking around, taking pictures, checking out the fallen-over windmill and water tank in the back, and I think I might have found a grave, but I'm not sure—there wasn't a headstone that I could see.

"I wanted to ride up the riverbed to the east to check out what was left of the corrals, barns, and other buildings, so I untied my horse, stepped into the saddle, and walked him about twenty feet toward the river. Then, out of the blue, comes a loud moaning sound from the house, and then a scream.

The horse jumps about three feet in the air and bucks me off.

"By the time I get up off the ground, he's tearing down the trail back to the ranch. I dusted myself off and looked back at the house. Everything was exactly the same as it was a minute before but, in the window on the second floor, there's somebody looking back at me.

"There's a woman standing in the window, in full view. She's dressed in a white dress with long sleeves and she's got long blond hair, and she's looking straight at me."

"You're not making this up, are you?" Jennifer asked.

"You didn't go to sleep on your horse, fall off, and are just covering it up?"

"No. Absolutely not. Honest. There was a woman in that window, all dressed in white—and she was looking at me."

CHAPTER 7

JANUARY 1873—TWO AND A HALF YEARS AFTER THE KIDNAPPING

"Tipton! You need to be up!" Tip woke with a start. He had felt the sheets as he snuggled deeper into them. He had seen the sun on the wallpaper of his room and the glittering dust in the morning air. He had heard the pots and pans clanking on the stove in the kitchen. He had smelled the pancakes and remembered the taste of fresh butter and warm milk.

But when he opened his eyes, the only light came from smoldering embers in the middle of the teepee, and the smells were only of dull smoke, dirt, body stink, and buffalo hair. The faint glow made shadows around the humps of women and children buried under mounds of thick, shaggy robes and wool blankets.

He was cold. Every morning, he was cold. Every evening, he was cold.

Winters were the hardest. The Comanche culture had molded itself to the sun and moon and thereby to sunlight and moonlight. When the nights were longer, they slept longer. When it was cold, they stayed in their teepees. But it was harder to hunt in the winter, and there were no plants to eat, so he was always hungry, and he was always cold.

More time to sleep also meant more time to dream…and to remember. He remembered the springs of his bed that squeaked when he moved and the sunlight in the window. He remembered his mother and father, even though he had a new father now and three new mothers whom he regarded highly and loved as he had loved the first. He had been told everything that had happened to his parents, to Lucy, to the ranch. Frontier people loved stories of hangings and suicides and such, and the Comancheros, the traders between Indians and the frontier people, carried the stories to the tribes. They spoke to the chief, and the chief had told the stories to Tip.

Two years? Or three years? Where had they been? There were violent snowstorms in the canyons of the Palo Duro the year he was taken. Then they traveled along the Llano into southern New Mexico, staying with the Apache.

They were in Mexico and then ranged to the north, where the big mountains provided long-term hiding places. One winter was in the land of deep snows. Then there was summer. Now they were somewhere in the north, near the Platte River, close to Sitting Bull's camp.

Two and a half years. He had been two and a half years living as a Comanche.

Rolling over and drawing the buffalo hide closer around his head, he could feel the thick braids of his hair. Red Hair, some called him. Hair of Red Clay, some called him. Head On Fire, some called him. When they captured him as a boy, his red hair was obvious, but they could not have expected his size. They had not seen his father and could not have known that the redheaded boy would grow like he had. Tip was as tall as any man in the village, even though he was only twelve. Or thirteen? No, a half-year past twelve. In the summer, he would be thirteen. He never knew the day, but he remembered the August moon.

He never had his party.

As he pulled the hide close around him, Tip knew that spring would come eventually, and he would not be so cold and hungry. Then he'd be hot again in summer, and fall would bring the colors, and it would all be good. Comanches molded themselves to the earth. Being part of the earth was their satisfaction and desire.

Tip stretched. He wished a woman were awake to bring him food.

It was a lot easier being a Comanche than being white, and easier being a male than a female. He did no chores.

The women did the chores. They gathered the wood, built the fires, did the cooking, skinned the buffalo and deer, dried the meat, made the clothes, hauled the water.

Comanche men practiced riding horses, stealing, shooting arrows, making fire, and fighting. The older men taught them the tactics of battle: the signals, the formations, the planning of war. Tip learned to make his own bows and arrows and to ride against his enemies, leaning to the side of his horse and firing an arrow under a horse's neck. He learned to track buffalo, deer, antelope, and elk, to call turkeys, and to lay traps for rabbits and raccoons.

Every day, he and his brothers played games and chased ponies and wrestled and played jokes on the older men.

Of course, he was the son of the chief—and it mattered that he was the son of the chief.

But it wasn't all fun. Sometimes, the chief would send them on raids. Long distances, many days gone, sometimes days before they could eat. They would travel far from camp, from the mountains into the plains, from the plains into the white settlements, from the settlements across the mountains into other mountains. They stole horses and mules to trade to the Comancheros for iron to make arrowheads, guns and ammunition, knives, blankets, and beads.

Sometimes, they revenged against the soldiers from the forts or the settlers who killed their buffalo or built houses in their territory. He hadn't killed any people. Yet. And he didn't think that he'd like killing people. But the stealing was fun. He was one of the best, and he already had many tales of sneaking through the darkness to lonely ranch corrals, slipping catches from gates, leading horses away, and laughing at the surprise of the settlers the next morning.

It mattered how many horses and mules you stole. It mattered that you did it well.

Then there were the hunts!

Tip smiled and felt pleasure in his heart. There weren't as many buffalo as there used to be, so they were harder to find, but when tracks were found, the whole village set out in pursuit. Every man in the village would spend a day painting himself, his shield, and his horse. They would dance that night, shuffling around and around the fire, jumping and yelling, working themselves into a frenzy. The next day, the chief arrayed the warriors against the buffalo as if in a war.

The sound of the herd! The smells! The feeling as he rode as fast as the wind, coming closer and closer to the hairy beasts snorting and thundering with their giant hooves, buckling to the earth when his spear or arrow found the heart. Then you whooped and shouted and grabbed another spear and went at them again.

Then everyone feasted and danced and whooped and celebrated.

It mattered how many buffalo you killed. It mattered that you did it well.

Tip reached over, laid another stick on the fire, disappeared under his hide, and slept.

CHAPTER 8

PRESENT DAY

t was Sunday morning at the Buffalo Skull, and the guests were moving out of their rooms, packing their cars, buying postcards from the ranch's gift shop, and suffering the dust as the cars drove out to the highway. After scurrying to clean up the brunch dishes, get the rooms refreshed, and tidy up the patio, Jennifer and the rest of the staff were still in motion when the new week's guests began arriving.

Jennifer had expected the Museum of the American Cowboy people to look like cowboys. Instead, they were university types, wearing T-shirts, shorts, and track shoes, each carrying smartphones, iPads, and laptops. Unloading their cars and SUVs resulted in piles of computers, printers, projectors, screens, books, posters, drawings, maps, photographs, and mounds of other materials.

"Pardon me, dear, but where does a lady pee around here?"

Jennifer turned to find a face hidden by more wrinkles than she could count, surrounding a pleasant smile. The woman was about her height, and thin, with white hair tied in a bun, leaning slightly on a cane. She wore a patterned, long-sleeve shirt with snaps rather than buttons, a worn—though clean and pressed—pair of jeans, and beautifully embroidered cowboy boots.

"Yes, Ma'am, right inside those double doors," Jennifer replied, directing the woman.

"Oh, good. Since you seem so nice, you won't mind escorting me over there, will you? The last few miles of dirt road gave my bladder a good working over, and I may need help getting the last few feet without an accident."

Jennifer had to smile as the woman took hold of her arm and strolled through the doors and into the restroom, all the while talking about the trip and how exciting the country looked.

"I've wanted to come here for many years," the woman continued, "but never quite made it. I'm from Montana, you see, and even though I've traveled many places, the wilds of New Mexico never quite made it on my agenda. Where are you from?"

After the bathroom, Jennifer walked the woman back to the van as she continued to talk.

Her name was Nedra Hamilton, she was seventy-five years old, and she was here with two other professors from the University of Montana. They were hoping to contribute some of their research on the northern routes of cattle drives and the subsequent growth of Montana cattle ranches. She also looked forward to tasting the famous green-chile enchiladas of New Mexico.

Jennifer was fascinated and overwhelmed at the same time. Professor Hamilton was a tireless talker, but also kind and cordial, with a ready smile. She was spry and quick-minded, and Jennifer couldn't help but laugh at her wit and humor. Between the two of them, they easily moved her luggage into her room in the hacienda—she didn't have much and was emphatic about not even owning a laptop.

"Thank you so much, dear," she said as she opened her room's door to the patio. "I believe I'll take a walk around the place."

She smiled pleasantly and looked Jennifer straight on.

"You'll be around, won't you? I'd like to get acquainted with the cowboys here, if we have a chance. Just the good-looking ones, of course," she said with a wink. "I only have a week.

"And the ranch operations? Maybe I can get a tour of how they manage the stock. We have quite a number of large cattle ranches in Montana, and I'd like to see how they do it in New Mexico."

Jennifer agreed that she could probably see as much of the ranch as she wanted and that she'd be most welcome to visit with Bud, the ranch manager. She excused herself to get back to her duties helping the other guests settle in.

"Thank you again, dear," Professor Hamilton said. "I just bet that you and I will have a good week together."

————

Mogi spent the day helping the staff clean the Jeeps, ATVs, daypacks, and other equipment used by the guests from the previous week and sorting them into their correct places in and around the equipment shed.

It was late Sunday evening when he and Jennifer sat together on the headquarters porch.

"She's really something," Jennifer said. "I didn't meet the others, but Professor Nedra Hamilton is certainly unique."

"I think I saw her," Mogi said. "The whole bunch has already staked out the patio for their discussions, and she was off to the side, watching the others set up their laptops and presentation stuff. For having a cane, she stands remarkably straight. Has Granddad met her?"

"I haven't seen him today. I think he and Bud have been going over autopsy reports from the dead cattle. I bet that once the presentations start, he'll find a way to sit in on some of them."

There was the sudden blaring of a horn as a pickup pulled into the hacienda parking lot. Clapping broke out from the group of museum guests on the patio and everyone stood up.

"Let's go see what's up," Mogi said as he stood and stepped off the porch.

It wasn't hard to identify the pickup being applauded.

It was a four-door, one-ton, dual-axle, four-wheel-drive monster that was painted a glowing crimson. Air horns from an eighteen-wheeler were mounted on the cab, the exhaust pipes ran up next to the cab, it had running lights across the front and down the sides, and on each door were giant insignias of the University of Oklahoma.

Mogi watched the driver step down from the cab. Almost as wide as he was tall, the man wore a huge cowboy hat, spurs with oversized rowels, and—putting them on as he finished off his outfit at the pickup door—a double-hung holster with two silver six-shooters.

Mogi thought that perhaps he had been hired as the entertainment for the evening, but as the man made his way to the patio, the applause increased.

"Oh, dear," Jennifer whispered, "I believe I was warned about this one. That's Dr. Lassiter Jones, the director of the museum."

Mogi stared in disbelief. "That's the director?"

"Oh, yeah. He's quite the character. Those guns are real, by the way, he's a believer in going armed. And the spurs are solid silver. I've been told that he made a huge amount of money in oil a long time before he got interested in art. But when he did, he bankrolled a private collection of Western art that's the envy of collectors around the world. He's got political connections as well, which is how he ended up being the director. Nice enough guy, I've heard, but definitely a character."

When the man reached the patio, he motioned with his hand and the applause subsided.

"And a mighty fine evening to all you buckaroos!" he shouted.

The crowd went crazy with laughter.

"Now, seriously, I apologize for being a little late, but the traffic on I-40 was like a buffalo herd on new grass. So, belatedly, I welcome you to our little retreat here and hope that you've already started warming up with some great discussions.

"You've all been given a rough agenda, but let me encourage you to take advantage of everything that the Buffalo Skull Ranch has to offer in the free time that we've scheduled. We'll take the cool of the mornings to have talks, take the afternoon off to play and take naps, then get back together after supper.

"I especially want to thank Bud and the ranch staff for having us"—there was hearty applause—"and I hope that each of you, as you sit around and talk about cowboy things, will remember that right out there"—he pointed west—"is where Charlie Goodnight was the first one to push Longhorns up to Colorado. We are in the very midst of history! Everybody have a good time!"

After another round of applause, the guests went back to their conversations.

CHAPTER 9

Jennifer tried to focus on the mattress instead of the pain that had taken up residence beneath her shoulder blades. Twisting to press a knot in her shoulder muscle, she grabbed the bottom sheet and jerked it off the bed and onto the floor.

Wrapping the used sheets in a loose ball, she stuffed them into the bag on her rolling cart, retrieved a clean set, and remade the bed, pulling the new sheets as tight as she could. She smoothed the bedspread into place, fluffed and arranged the pillows, and placed two chocolate mints on top.

The rooms were all decorated in Santa Fe style: Log beams, or *vigas*, ran across the ceiling from wall to wall, with white plaster between. The walls were heavily stuccoed to give a rough, adobe-like texture, and small Navajo rugs of bright reds and blues hung around the room. The king-sized bed had no foot-board, but the headboard was made of ornately carved wood with a New Mexico sun symbol in the center. A wooden desk, with intricate lines of carved patterns running up each leg, was arranged in a corner with a matching chair.

The bedspread was a Native American pattern of blues and greens. The polished red bricks of the floor gave a warm, comfortable feeling to the room, and the carved, wooden side tables were topped with bright Mexican tiles. A small oval fireplace was built into the corner of the room, and a basket of firewood sat nearby.

Jennifer sighed. Now it was time for the bathroom.

It was only Wednesday morning, but Jennifer was already feeling worn out by the grueling pace of her housekeeping duties. Breakfast was set out at six for the ranch hands and staff, and then cleaned up. Breakfast at the hacienda was from seven to nine, with less food to prepare, but the guests took longer, and clean-up couldn't be started until they were finished.

After helping with breakfast, Jennifer cleaned and refreshed the rooms. Then she helped with lunch, cleaned the hacienda common areas, swept and tidied the patio, helped with supper, and on and on. There was a two-hour period in the afternoon that the staff had to themselves, but it was nowhere near the time she needed to recover.

She kept a smile on her face and was on her best behavior, but she was tired and sore and sure her back would never be straight again. She knew that riding a horse all day was hard, but she often envied her brother for being outside.

And if her undercover work was supposed to turn up any potential enemies of the ranch, she was failing miserably.

The staff members she'd met were content and liked their jobs, the cowboys and cowgirls she'd met were laid back and happy despite all the hard work they did, and everybody loved Bud. Since the guests were at the ranch for such a short time, she assumed that none of them could be connected to the cattle deaths.

Jennifer finished cleaning the toilet, the tub, and the sink, dragged a Swiffer over the floor, straightened the towels, and ran a vacuum over the small floor rugs. A senior staffer would come in later to check everything, so she was careful to make everything as neat and clean as possible.

"There's just the girl I'm looking for," a voice called out behind her.

It was Nedra Hamilton. "I hope you're not in love with housework because I'm going to spirit you away for a special project."

Jennifer started to list the rooms she had left to do, but Professor Hamilton brushed her objections aside. "I've already talked to your supervisor, and I've even talked to Bud, so it will be fine for you to let it all go," she said with a twinkle in her eye. She leaned closer as if to share a secret. "At my age, all you have to do is act old and feeble, and it's amazing what people will do for you. Of course, it helps to look like everyone's grandmother."

She laughed.

"So, I'm going to carry you off for some excitement, if you don't mind. I'll miss the presentations, but more than half of those researchers wouldn't know a steer if it stepped on them, so it's hard to believe that they know what they're talking about. It's time for a little escape."

Jennifer turned her cart over to another staff member. She tried to smile innocently, as if she was sorry to give up her duties. In reality, she was overjoyed to do something different.

Professor Hamilton guided her outside to a patio table and sat down.

"Now, dear, I believe you have a brother who's seen a ghost?"

Jennifer wasn't sure how to respond. Wasn't it supposed to be a secret? Who else knew?

"Uh, well, I'm not...ah, okay. I do have a brother, and he believes that he recently saw a ghost."

Professor Hamilton clapped her hands and laughed. "It's so nice to have someone who admits to what they know. And, if my sources are correct, he saw this ghost at the Mulvaney Castle, is that right?"

"Yes, Ma'am. I've not been there, so the details will have to come from him."

"Well, I expected. So, instead of imagining the famous castle, I would like for us to see it. And, as I see your brother and his long legs striding across the parking lot, I believe he's been told that he gets to be our tour guide."

———

Professor Nedra Hamilton had to be one of the funniest people they had ever met.

After getting over the initial shock of being publicly recognized for being ghostbusters, the Franklin siblings, with Jennifer driving one of the ranch SUVs, were enjoying the seemingly endless tales Professor Hamilton told as they drove along.

She recounted the relationship between Charlie Goodnight and his best friend, Oliver Loving, and the painful story of Loving's death from a wound suffered in an Indian fight. After finishing the cattle drive that they were both on, Goodnight returned to take his friend's body eight hundred miles back to his home in Texas, where Loving could be buried with Masonic honors.

She told of the Lincoln County wars, Billy the Kid, Pat Garrett, John Chisum, and, as they drew closer to Las Vegas, of the rip-snorting, rip-roaring frontier town that it once was, with the likes of Wyatt Earp, Doc Holliday, Bat Masterson, Black Jack Ketchum, Kit Carson, and a string of other names they recognized from the Old West.

"Besides the brothels and the bars, the local *patron* ruled the sheriff and the judge, so the liquor flowed freely, as well as the bullets. Las Vegas gave Santa Fe a run for its money when it came to corruption."

It took an hour to drive from the ranch to Las Vegas.

Ten minutes north of the small city, they took a turnoff from Interstate-25 and then drove another hour before dropping into the Mora River canyon and pulling around to the castle.

Mogi offered to recite the details of his encounter, but Professor Hamilton had put him off until she could see the house for herself. Now, as they pulled around in front of the sad, broken-down ruin, Professor Hamilton was surprisingly quiet.

In fact, she seemed unable to talk. She stepped from the front seat of the SUV, closed the door, and carefully picked her way across the front yard. Standing before the crumbling structure, looking up at the house, she put her hands lightly to her lips and stared.

It was a full five minutes before the professor seemed ready to continue. Reaching for Jennifer's arm, the two slowly made their way around the house, carefully stepping between pieces of slate, piles of wood, rocks, sand drifts, brush, and tumbleweeds. Still not saying anything, almost in a trance, the elderly woman focused on the house as if waiting for permission to enter.

Mogi found another board to widen the walkway he created on his first visit to the house, hoping to make it easier for the professor to make it up the slope.

Finally, in a voice almost too quiet for Jennifer to hear, the woman said, "It must be done, it must," and stepped onto the plank leading to the front of the house.

Slowly, carefully, deliberately, Nedra Hamilton walked her way into Mulvaney Castle.

Jennifer and Mogi were now both intensely watching the woman. They could hear her increased breathing and muttered sighs and saw her hands grow shaky. Exchanging glances, they both held on to her as she began a shuffling journey through the inside doors.

The silence was broken as a moan began—low, like a long-held bass note, and then a vibration and a prolonged hiss of air, as if the house itself were sighing.

Mogi's hair stood straight up on the back of his neck.

Jennifer's heart pounded.

"Ohhhh..." the professor uttered. She quivered, stiffened, and gave a small cry as she slumped to the floor.

CHAPTER 10

"I'm afraid that I have not been completely open about myself," Professor Hamilton said as Jennifer stacked extra pillows behind her so she could sit up in bed.

After her collapse, Mogi and Jennifer scrambled to get Nedra back into the SUV. She came around soon enough and seemed to be fully herself by the time they had driven out of the canyon. But, still scared out of their wits, Mogi and Jennifer kept silent on the way back.

"I want to thank you, first of all," the professor continued as she sat up straight, "for putting up with my hard-headedness. You have been darlings, the both of you, and I do sincerely appreciate it. I should tell you, though, that I thought something like this might happen."

Mogi and Jennifer looked at each other in disbelief.

"But I needed to go into the house regardless of

how I might react. Though I have few beliefs in ghosts or spirits, I thought, just a little bit, that the house might recognize me."

"Recognize you?" Mogi and Jennifer exclaimed in unison.

"Yes. And it did. I don't know exactly how, but I felt like I was being squeezed like a frantic mother might squeeze a lost child. I know this is hard to believe, but the blood in that house is my blood. A part of me was coming home, and the house knew it." She took a deep breath. "I am Lucy Mulvaney's great-granddaughter."

It took a moment for Mogi's mind to interpret what she had said. Lucy Mulvaney. Martin Mulvaney. Lucy.

Okay, Lucy Mulvaney was the six-year-old daughter of Martin Mulvaney, the child who was sent back east to relatives after her mother had lost her mind.

"Lucy was the daughter who was sent away," Jennifer said.

"The sister of the boy who was kidnapped," Mogi added.

"Yes. There's a side to the story of Mulvaney Castle that only a few know. I am one of them, and perhaps the only one who has ever cared. If I may, I would like to tell you that story."

"Of course," Jennifer said as Mogi vigorously nodded his head. He pulled a desk chair over to the bed and Jennifer sat on the edge of the mattress.

"I've known the story of Martin Mulvaney and his

family most of my life. In fact, from the time I was in mid-school, I had heard stories of the murderous ancestor who killed his partner, and his wife, who committed suicide. Evil ancestors in the family are so enjoyable when you're a budding young girl—it lends such an aura of mystery to your life.

"However, there was one part of the story that stayed with me, a part that begged for a little more resolution than just family gossip. Mogi, dear, would you hand me my briefcase?"

The professor opened the case, searched through some files, and retrieved a laminated piece of yellow paper. "Let me tell you the complete story," she said.

"Lucy Mulvaney was six years old when the Comanches kidnapped her brother, Tipton. It was, in fact, on the morning of Tipton's tenth birthday, August 10, 1870. A month or so later, Martin Mulvaney, the father, recognized that his delicate wife's mental condition was rapidly failing, so he booked passage for Lucy and a housekeeper on the train that ran from Trinidad, Colorado, to St. Louis, Missouri, intending that Lucy be given over to his wife's brother and sister-in-law until such time that he and Violet could join her.

"Did you know that Martin's wife's name was Violet? She was my great-great-grandmother.

"Well, Lucy and the housekeeper traveled by stage from Las Vegas to Trinidad, then on by various trains. They arrived in St. Louis on September 29. Unfortunately, by that time, her father had murdered his ex-partner and was hanged and buried, and her mother had disappeared. The information had been telegraphed to Violet's brother before Lucy ever stepped through their door.

"Knowing this information about their demise just deepened the distance between the two families. Violet's brother and sister-in-law, in fact, already hated Martin Mulvaney for taking Violet to a rough, uncouth frontier they mistakenly believed was full of heathen white men and flesh-eating savages.

"As soon as the two arrived, the housekeeper was fired and ordered out of the state, and Lucy was taken ferociously to their breasts. They adopted her as quickly as possible to erase the Mulvaney name from her memory and never told her the truth about what happened to her parents. She was told they had died of cholera. Her brother, Tipton, was seldom, if ever, mentioned, and always in the past tense—he was certainly dead.

"Lucy Mulvaney, now named Lucille Simpson, ultimately had a normal childhood in a wealthy home and never heard another word of her true family beyond what little she could remember. Nothing happened that would have brought the truth to light.

"Until 1879. In May of 1879, this arrived at the Simpson house."

Professor Hamilton held out the piece of yellow paper and both Mogi and Jennifer huddled around it. It measured about five by seven inches and had the words *Western Union* across the top.

"It's a telegram," she said. "The lettering is quite faded, but if you turn it over, you can see an enhanced copy of what it says stapled to the back. The telegram was sent by *Mr. Smith* from Las Vegas, New Mexico Territories, on May 6, 1879, to Lucy Mulvaney, in care of Neville Simpson, Violet's brother. It had only three words: *Run, Lucy, Run.*

"You might expect that something this unusual would be received with great curiosity, and people would want to know what it meant. In fact, Lucy, who was now fourteen or fifteen, had been sent to a boarding school in Chicago in the fall and was not even home when it arrived.

"Instead of wondering about the meaning of the telegram, the Simpsons put it into an envelope and discreetly shoved it away in a back drawer, and that was the end of it. Any use of the name Mulvaney was not to be paid attention to. Lucy never saw the telegram nor even knew of its existence.

"Many years later, in 1930, when Lucy was herself a grandmother, her adoptive parents died and, in their records, the envelope was found.

"The details are few, but I know this much: Lucy, surrounded by friends who were helping to sort through the Simpsons' belongings, opened the envelope, read the telegram, and suddenly screamed. She stood straight up, as if hit by a lightning bolt. She continued to scream, then cried, then staggered, and then collapsed, as dead as if the devil himself had snatched her soul that very instant.

"After she died, the family began an investigation, and that's when the truth about the Mulvaney family came to light. Nothing, however, was found that explained the telegram's three words, nor Lucy's deadly shock when she read them."

Mogi and Jennifer sat silently, glancing from Nedra Hamilton's face to the sparsely worded telegram on the bed in front of them.

Run, Lucy, Run.

CHAPTER 11

Friday evening finally came.

The clouds over the mountains to the west were large and billowing but quickly thinned out to stretch over the horizon. The setting sun gave their undersides a spectrum of reds, oranges, and yellows, with bright, golden edges as they caught the last rays of sunlight. The hacienda's adobe finish took on a warm golden glow, the shade softening from the large cottonwoods overhead.

Everything began to slowly cool down as the light faded.

Mogi and Jennifer stood next to a corral fence, watching the horses roll in the dust and sprint around after a hard workday. Mogi felt like he also needed a good roll in the dust. It had been a long week.

He began his fence riding early Monday morning, looking for broken or loose wire. After checking a section, he would take a side trip, looking into canyons, locating different windmills and water tanks, searching for any clues about wrongdoings or out-of-place vehicles. He paid special attention to any disturbance of the vegetation, in case someone was spraying the grass with poisonous substances, the water, in case someone was trying to contaminate it, and suspicious tracks, in case someone was spying on specific herds.

The Wednesday trip to the Mulvaney Castle had given him a break, but the story about Lucy and the unusual telegram replayed itself in his brain all evening, enough that he welcomed his routine on Thursday. By Friday afternoon, he'd worked all of the fence on the Canadian River side of the ranch and was back at headquarters.

He had found nothing unusual.

Jennifer's Thursday and Friday were a repeat of the first part of the week. She still had Saturday to look forward to, and then she'd get Sunday off. Again, she found no one unhappy or disgruntled, no hint of problems.

It had rained twice. A cloudy day on Tuesday provided a slow, gentle rain that soaked the plains and brought an overnight burst of green across the basin floor. Thursday began cloudless, but the afternoon brought a quick build-up of clouds that drenched the ranch, with miniature tsunamis running down the dirt roads.

Jennifer had watched the cloudburst from inside the hacienda, but Mogi was caught out on his horse in the middle of a pasture, groping to keep his hat on and, at the same time, trying to keep the wind from blowing his slicker open. For all his efforts, he still ended up with a wet crotch for the rest of the day.

"How are your feet?" he asked Jennifer.

"You cowboys can keep your boots, I'm going back to my sandals. The inch and a half I gain from these still keeps me looking up at people, so I don't even get to feel tall like you do."

Mogi stretched his arms across the top rail of the corral, arched his back to work out a cramp, and sighed.

"Hey, you two!" Granddad called as he walked across the barnyard toward them.

"Long time no see!" Jennifer called. "We're just resting up from the week."

At Granddad's request, Mogi went through a list of the week's happenings—working the fence, Professor Hamilton, the visit to the castle, and Lucy Mulvaney's story. He opened his phone and showed him the picture he had taken of the telegram.

"Now that's a puzzle, for sure," Granddad commented as he looked it over. "And nobody guessed who Mr. Smith was? The message hardly seems like something that would cause a heart attack."

"Any progress on the cattle losses?" Mogi asked.

"None. It's been a week since the last death, and the coroners have turned up nothing. They don't have a clue what's going on."

"What did you do in Santa Fe?"

"Well, let's see," Granddad said. "The whole point of the trip was to see if I could find any business or individual who would benefit from the Buffalo Skull going under or if there was any news about an oil, gas, wind, solar, or environmental group that might be holding a grudge against the ranch, the owners, Bud, or anybody else connected to it.

"I looked through newspapers, I talked to reporters, I visited some financial people in Albuquerque, I visited some old ranchers in Las Vegas, and it all amounted to nothing. Well, let's see, I take that back. The one bit of information that's new is that somebody has offered to buy the ranch."

"What? Who?"

"Well, we don't know. Bud was told by the owners that Sotheby's International, the big auction house and real estate company, had been contacted about an offer, but they wouldn't tell him who made the offer. The offer is $50 million, which is about half what the owners think the ranch is worth. Bud laughed it off, but the owners are a lot more scared since the cattle started dying."

"You think the owners might sell?" Mogi asked. "It's weird to think about selling the whole ranch. That's a half-million acres."

"I don't know," Granddad answered. "About a year ago, somebody made the same kind of offer, and the owners didn't even bother to respond. But now, if cattle keep dying, and they can't find a cause, the state might require all the cattle to be destroyed, and no animals could be raised on the ranch for at least a year. If that happened, $50 million would look awfully good. If the owners didn't sell, it could take years to rebuild the herds and the breeding programs."

Their three faces looked glum at the prospect.

"Hey," Jennifer said, trying to change the subject. "Have you been able to attend any of the talks? This cattle drive stuff and all the stories of the cowboys sound pretty interesting."

"I've caught a few in the mornings," Granddad replied, "and boy, do I wish I had more time for them. Just watching Lassiter Jones is worth the price of admission. That guy is something. He really loves this stuff—talks about the old cattle kings of the West, like Goodnight, John Chisum, Jesse Chisholm, and the early frontier life with the Texas Rangers.

"He gave a talk one morning about what it meant to be a scout for a cattle drive—what it took in terms of personality, strength, endurance, path finding, knowledge, wisdom, and even how good their eyesight had to be. Ol' Lassiter had you sweating at the dangers one moment and saluting the flag the next. He might look like window-dressing, but he's got a cowboy's head and heart, that's for sure.

"Well, I'm going to go soak in the hot tub. By the way, you won't want to miss tomorrow night."

"Saturday! Time for the chuckwagon feed, yee haw!" Mogi said, remembering the all-you-can-eat spread.

"Actually, no," Granddad replied. "Bud was telling me that a few of the historians have offered to treat the ranch to what a *real* chuckwagon supper would have looked like. They're going to use only what was available on cattle drives in the 1860s, which means everything has to be cooked over a fire, either in a cast-iron pot or on a spit.

"Bud's going to give them a calf to kill, and there's a group going hunting tomorrow for rabbits, snakes, and turtles. You can bet on a few gallons of beans, plus they've got a recipe for preparing cactus that's a hundred years old. They've even got a stew recipe that Charlie Goodnight himself created. He was so particular about how it was made that he'd fire the cook if any ingredient were ever left out.

"But the best thing is the main course. They're going to cook the calf's head, which they say was quite a delicacy at the time."

"Oh, that's gross!" Jennifer cried. "Leave me out of this. I'm not eating anything that's looking back at me."

"Well, that's your choice. Meanwhile, I'm off for a while. See you two tomorrow." Granddad strolled back to headquarters.

"Cooking the calf's head? Do you think he was kidding?" Mogi asked.

"I don't even want to think about it," Jennifer responded.

Mogi still had his phone in his hand. "You want to see the photographs I took when I went to the castle the first time? You didn't get much of a chance to see it on Wednesday."

"Sure, but I need to sit for a while. My whole body hurts."

They retreated to the patio, where Mogi pulled up two chairs.

"I'll skip some of the early shots," he said, swiping through the photos. He brought up the S curve and then stopped at the first picture of the old house.

"Which window did you see the woman in?" Jennifer asked.

Mogi pointed, zoomed in, and then moved to the pictures of the inside of the house.

"That's the famous fireplace. The inside walls keep you from seeing the whole thing, but walking through the doorways shows that it must be twelve feet square or bigger. Here's the kitchen…a view into the back-yard…the staircase up to the second floor…the bathroom. I wonder if they had one of those cast-iron tubs with claw feet. And here's the room that has the window…and the stairway up to the attic.

"After going through the inside, I walked around the house and took pictures of each side of the house and the windmill out back. They're farther away from where you were the other day, so these might give you a better perspective."

He expanded each picture. The fallen porch formed a rippling pile of wood across the ground. The porch's roof sections had either fallen off or were hanging against the side of the house like a ripped sail from an old boat. The stone covering on the outside was in remarkably good shape, and the slate roof, though swaybacked in a couple of places, looked secure.

"That's kind of cute," Jennifer said.

"What?"

"That window sticking out of the roof. The way that it's curved along the top instead of being straight."

Mogi looked at it closely.

"I don't remember any window like that," he said, using his fingers to enlarge the picture.

The window was small, maybe only a foot or so tall, but instead of belonging to a room inside the house, the window was part of the roof itself, with the roof lifting up and arching over it the way an eyebrow arches over an eye.

"Hmm. I'm sure that there was no window like that inside the house," Mogi said thoughtfully. "I wonder if it's in the roof behind the walls of one of the attic rooms?"

"Is the glass still in the window?" Jennifer asked.

"There's something reflecting off the surface, and what's that stuff to the right?"

Mogi enlarged the image more and looked again.

"Holy cow! Not only does it look like there's still glass in it, but do you see what I see?"

In the corner of the window was a whitish blur behind the bare wood of the window casing. Along the edge of the blur a number of lines twisted in and around the edge.

Lace.

"That's a curtain!"

———

"Can you do it?" Mogi asked anxiously.

"Won't be a problem," his sister answered. "The museum bunch has been taking care of themselves. They're even skipping Saturday lunch to get ready for the cattle drive dinner tomorrow night. After the rooms are cleaned in the morning, I'm free the rest of the day. I'll probably have to work on Sunday, though."

"Great! We'll get somebody to give us a ride out to Camp Six, and Mr. Valdez will let us borrow a couple of horses for the day. Then we can go investigate our little window. There's no glass left in any of the other windows of the house, much less any curtains, so that window must be someplace that nobody could have gotten to from inside the house. Or maybe there's a panel or hidden door that accesses the dead space under the roof."

"So, I get to ride a horse?"

"I'll choose 'im myself, ma'am," Mogi said with a smile. "Just remember they don't come with seatbelts."

———

"Y'all have a good ride," Hector Valdez said as he adjusted the stirrups to fit Jennifer. "Keep an eye on the river. There was a pretty good storm over the mountains by Las Vegas the last couple of days, so the river will probably be up a foot or so. I've tied on slickers, so if a frog-strangler comes in, move away from the river and trees and hunker down until it moves on. Don't worry about the horses—they're drip-dry."

"Yes, sir. We appreciate your help."

Mogi and Jennifer left the corral at a slow walk, but once away from the fences, Mogi brought the horses to a soft lope.

"AAHHH!" Jennifer cried as she held on tight to the saddle horn.

Mogi laughed. "Sit up straight and try to keep your head steady. Let your lower body rock along with the horse. Imagine that you're pushing your knees into his shoulders."

Thankfully, it wasn't long until they reached the bottom of the cliffs and rode into the canyons, slowing to a walk as they followed the trail around the curving river.

The water was a little higher at the crossing than Mogi remembered, but it was no problem for the horses to push their way through. In a few minutes, they plodded up a rise in the river's bank.

Mulvaney Castle stood right in front of them.

CHAPTER 12

Mogi looked up at the window on the second floor.

Nothing.

He hadn't expected the ghost to be there, but he wished Jennifer could see it, she'd know he hadn't imagined it. The moan and hiss when Nedra Hamilton collapsed certainly showed that strange things were happening, but he figured Jennifer needed to see the woman to actually believe him. And maybe he needed to see her again to believe it himself. He also wanted to know if the house was going to moan again. Would the house remember them from when the professor was here?

He dismounted, helped Jennifer down, and led the two horses into the yard. He tied the reins around a remnant of a porch support.

"Shall we take a look?" Jennifer said. She couldn't help but be wary about the strange happenings. She believed her brother about the ghost, but on the other hand, really?

What did a woman in a white dress have anything to do with her brother? And why now? But throw in Nedra Hamilton's experience and there was no question there was something funny about this house. What would she do if she actually saw a ghost?

The little eyebrow window—now that was something she was interested in, something that was physical and could be touched. It wasn't often she noticed anything that her brother had missed, so its value was already high.

Maybe it would lead them to a secret room. That would definitely be cool.

Mogi brought the picture up on his phone. Walking around to the side and looking up, he backed away from the house to see the roof.

It was right there. The tiny window was dwarfed by the slate shingles on both sides and the massive chimney behind it, so it wasn't surprising he had missed it.

It was a good distance away, but with binoculars, they could tell that the original white paint had worn off the outside trim, the glass was intact, and there was the faintest hint of lace on the other side.

"Okay. We have a mystery window on the outside that we don't see on the inside. But it has to show up somewhere inside, doesn't it? All we have to do is find it, right?"

Jennifer watched her brother as he used his hands to estimate distances across the roof. Using the chimney as a reference, he imagined marking off the distances on the inside of the house.

She wandered off.

"So, inside," Mogi said, now talking to himself, "it should be pretty easy to go to the second-story window that's closest to the front of the house and walk back that way about ten feet. If there's no access to under the roof, then we have to go up to the attic rooms. It has to be there someplace."

But what was supposed to be pretty easy turned out to be pretty difficult.

Inside the room on the second floor, Mogi walked from the edge of the window along the outside wall. He could only go six feet before he hit a wall. Looking at the ceiling, there was no access upward. Moving to the next room was no different—no indication of any access.

Going up the closet stairway put him into the small attic rooms. Pacing across the floor, he guessed where the windows were below him. Again, the room wasn't big enough to go ten more feet in the direction of where he was sure the little window would be. He tried the same in the small hallway. He knew he wasn't even close. He looked for an opening or door or panel that would allow him into the space beneath the roof but found nothing.

The only explanation was that the window was in the empty space between the rooms and the roof. But there was no opening into that area. Why would you put a window where you couldn't get to it and then put a curtain on it?

————

While her brother was pondering the problems of space and time, Jennifer had walked up the plank walkway and was exploring the house.

She had hesitated at the front door but took a deep breath and stepped through. There was no moan, no hiss, no hug when she passed through the door. Nothing. So that was good, she figured, and continued.

It must have been a grand house, she thought, looking at the huge rooms built for entertaining. The living room alone could have held twenty or more people standing around in their fine clothes, being sociable. The kitchen could have held several cooks and servants at a time, and the dining room was big enough for a table that might have sat fifteen or twenty.

What parties they must have had! She envisioned the stairways with polished oak treads and banisters, with the side windows letting the sunlight shine down the stairwells. I bet they even had stained glass windows! she thought. And a piano! And enough room for dancing!

The bedrooms would have held four-poster beds, armoires for storing clothes, and probably one of those dressers where the woman sat in the middle with three mirrors around her. Large rugs in bright reds, yellows, browns, and greens would have been placed throughout the house, and Jennifer bet that every window downstairs had lace curtains, with more sturdy broadcloth in the bedrooms.

She carefully stepped down the edges of the stairway treads and walked through the front room to an outside window. Soft pellets of water were hitting the surface of the porch rubble outside. The view across the river had softened from bright sunlight to a darker tone.

"Hey! Hey up there! Did you know it's raining?"

She heard the thumps of Mogi's boots as he moved across the floor above and down the attic stairs. Then she heard him cross and step carefully down onto the first floor. He came through a doorway and walked across to join her at the window.

"How hard is it..." was as much as he could say before the view outside the window lit up with an explosive flash. A half-second later, a massive *boom* surrounded them as the house shook. The sound quickly moved across the yard, across the riverbed, and echoed back along the canyon walls.

Mogi yelled in surprise and leaped across the room.

"I've got to get the horses!" he yelled at Jennifer as he jumped through the doorway. "Meet me around back!"

The two horses were wide-eyed and terrified, jerking against their reins, shivering their manes, and stamping their hooves. Mogi grabbed each horse by the bridle and yanked the reins off the upright. Wrapping the reins around his hand and holding hard from the hip, he pulled the horses back from the porch and struggled to hold them as they nervously banged against each other. Finally, they quieted enough to be led to the back of the house.

Tying them to the fallen-over windmill, he ran to Jennifer as she watched from the kitchen doorway.

"The doorway here is a lot closer to the ground than the front," he yelled over the growing patter of the rain.

"Help me build a ramp. We'll get the horses inside the house and away from the lightning."

Several large sections of the porch roof lay close to the back door, heavy with slate but movable. Pushing and pulling and propping up the sides with broken timbers from the porch floor, they made a usable ramp. With the wind whipping raindrops into his face, Mogi ran to one horse, untied it, led it to Jennifer, and handed her the reins. With him behind, she led the horse up as easily as into a horse trailer. He did the same with the other horse.

The rain changed to hail as the wind howled down the canyon.

"We've got to keep them away from the windows and from where the floor has fallen in!" Mogi yelled as the pounding of the hail on the porch boards outside grew to a roar. The slate on the roof and the rock exterior kept most of the sound outside, but the unglazed window openings let hail stones come through and bounce across the floor like machine gun fire.

The horses kept shuffling their feet back and forth across the floor, trying to rear up but hitting their heads against the ceiling. Mogi looked in vain for a place to tie their reins to hold their heads down. Pulling them from one room to the other, he kept talking to them, trying to calm them.

A second bolt of lightning hit.

It must have been close. As the flash of light came through the windows, Mogi could see terror reflected in the horses' eyes. Their reins pulled out of his hands at about the same time the *boom* broke across the room.

There was no holding them now.

Both horses began bucking, ramming their heads into the ceiling, kicking at anything that was close, swinging their stirrups against the walls. Stamping the floor, circling around and butting into each other, the horses gave way to panic.

"Get out of the way!" Mogi yelled at his sister as he dove through a doorway.

The horses bucked through the doorways and into every room, scared into a frenzy of terror as the noise of the hail, the whipping of the wind, and more flashes and booms drove them crazy. Their horseshoes ripped scars across the old wood floors, and vicious kicks drove their back hooves into walls, against the stone of the chimney, the bookcases, and door frames. Shattered wood and plaster flew everywhere.

Working his way back to the kitchen, Mogi's horse jumped out the doorway and onto the ramp, leaped across the grass, and headed away at a gallop. The second horse followed.

Mogi and Jennifer were wide-eyed and breathing hard as they ran to the door opening, the wind and rain blowing into their faces. Stunned, they watched silently as both horses trampled through several inches of hail and dashed for the river. A few seconds later, they were gone from sight.

"Will they be all right?" Jennifer shouted, trying to catch her breath.

"I expect they will," Mogi replied, mad at himself for what now looked like foolish decisions. "I should have left them alone. Those horses are a lot smarter than I am and will be home a lot sooner than we'll be. Looks like a long walk back. I should never have brought them into the house!"

"Well, look at the bright side," Jennifer said as she tried to cheer up her brother. "Our food was tied in the slickers. Now, not only can you feel awful, you can be hungry, too."

The hail had quit, but raindrops continued to bombard the house and yard. Leaning against the chimney in the front room, Mogi and Jennifer looked out the doorway and windows with nothing to say.

Jennifer shivered and drew closer to her brother. It had gotten colder as the hail and rain quickly doused the heat captured in the soil and rock.

The floor began to shake a little, and a faint roar came through the windows.

The roar grew louder.

"More thunder?" Jennifer guessed.

Mogi shook his head. "I don't think so. Maybe we should get out of the house. It might be falling down."

They trotted down the ramp at the back of the house and made for the east side of the yard, where it was flat.

The rain had stopped, but the roar grew louder.

The water in the river had turned from clear to a murky brown. It began to swell in height, with waves splashing hard against the banks. Suddenly, Mogi and Jennifer could see a wall of water coming down the river valley.

"Flashflood!" Jennifer yelled as they sprinted for the cliffs behind the house. Up river, a monstrous wall of water rose out of the riverbed as it squirted through the narrow canyon walls of the Mora River. When it hit the Canadian, a huge spray of water launched straight out of the riverbed and smacked into the opposite canyon wall.

Rolling over and cascading back to the riverbed, the waters of the Canadian joined in to make a massive wave that headed for the narrow canyon of the S curve.

The water behind the front wave surged toward the house.

Mogi and Jennifer, out of breath with their hearts beating like bass drums, scrambled back and forth up the rock piles at the bottom of the cliffs until they reached a flat, shallow shelf of rock about twenty feet above the house's backyard. They sat down clumsily and watched with wide eyes as the huge waves washed down the canyon.

It did not last long. Behind the waves, the water broadened into the flatter land along the banks, becoming more shallow and slower. The power of the flashflood was lost.

The water calmed and slowly receded from the house's yard.

Mogi and Jennifer sat on their ledge, taking deep breaths and letting their hearts slow down.

"Look!" Jennifer gasped as she pointed toward the house.

There was a woman standing in the second-story window.

CHAPTER 13

The clouds began to thin and the increasing light beat back the darkness, but the shivers that Mogi and Jennifer felt in their already cold bodies were not from the temperature of the air.

They stared at the woman who stared at them, her face anxious. Her white dress, with its high lace neck, lace-covered sleeves, and lace bodice that led to many folds of satin, hung loosely on her slight frame. It was no doubt a wedding dress. Her hair, gathered on top in a Victorian fashion, hung in waves past her shoulders to frame her face, which was pretty but gaunt, her cheekbones covered with too little skin. Her eyes appeared sad and lonely.

Mogi and Jennifer were unable to move, both afraid that if they did, the apparition might fade. Against the fear that they might see her was now the desire that she not go away.

The woman's arms had been at her side, but she

suddenly raised one as if in farewell. Then she faded back into the darkness of the house.

———

"So, what do we do now?" Jennifer asked.

Mustering their courage, they had crept up the ramp to the back door and gone inside. The ground floor looked like a demolition site. Several walls had large holes in the shape of horses' hooves, door casings were broken, and there was even a hole through the back of the chimney bookcase in the kitchen. Broken plaster lay scattered across the floors in every room.

It looked like a war had been fought and lost.

Upstairs, they found nothing that showed the woman had been there.

After the flashflood, they had warmed up in the sunshine, walked the river to see the damage along the riverbanks, inspected the front yard that was now covered in mud, and checked out the remains of the corrals and outbuildings. Now they sat in the front doorway, absorbing what little sunlight was still coming over the cliffs to their west. It was about six o'clock, almost six hours since they'd left the ranch.

"All we can do is wait, like we already decided," Mogi responded with a shrug. "We sit. Mr. Valdez knows where we are, so Bud and Granddad know where we are. When the horses show up at the ranch with all of our stuff, they'll know that we don't have supplies. With the reins dragging the ground, I think they'll figure out that the horses came untied, so I don't think they'll worry about us having had an accident.

"I'm sure the canyon trail back to the ranch is flooded, or at least covered with enough mud that we could never slog our way through it. If we walk out by the road, it could be miles before we found another ranch or farm. It would be after midnight before we could get to any place. I'm sure Granddad will figure things out and take care of it from his end, so let's just wait. They'll be along directly."

He hadn't finished the sentence before they both heard a whining sound coming from the sky.

"See? I told ya!" Mogi exclaimed.

Bud's airplane appeared over the canyon rim and made a run past the house. Mogi and Jennifer waved and jumped up and down and Bud and Granddad waved back. Circling again and coming in lower, Granddad pushed a big bag out the door. It almost made it to the riverbank, splashing down in the shallows.

Mogi made a flying leap from the bank, caught it, and dragged it ashore. The airplane pulled out of the canyon and started circling.

It was an old Army duffle bag. Inside were two sleeping bags, jackets, a battery-operated lantern, a first-aid kit, a cardboard box full of food, and bottles of water. Taped to the box was a scribbled note:

Bottom canyon trail washed out, so no can do horses.
Upper road washed out at I-25 but should be able to get
through tomorrow morning. Signal if everything is okay
until then. We will figure out something else if not.

The airplane dipped again into the canyon and
flew low overhead. Jennifer and Mogi gave them a
thumbs-up and the plane lifted out of the canyon and
over the rim.

"I'm starving," Mogi said as he sat back down in
the doorway and opened the box. There were more
sandwiches than they could eat, some chips, and a
dozen cookies. It took only a few minutes for the
supplies to be reduced to a few choice items left for
breakfast.

"It's going to be dark soon," Jennifer said, "so we
have to decide where to sleep. Who votes for staying
in the haunted house?"

Mogi looked thoughtful.

"I've seen the woman two times," he said, "and I've
never felt in danger or threatened. She's never made a
move. I wonder if she would contact us if she could. If
we made beds right in the center of the living
room…"

"Are you nuts?" Jennifer shouted. "I was joking!
You would actually spend the night in here? I'm
looking over my shoulder every two seconds as it is!
I'm sleeping as far away from this house as I can,
assuming I'm going to sleep at all, that is."

"Uh, well," Mogi stammered, "you may have a valid

point about not sleeping. But...there's something here, some secret, some clue to the mysteries. I think she's trying to tell us something. Maybe she's a ghost that's lost in the spirit dimension and she's trapped, can't get out, can't make it to heaven or wherever, and she needs our help, you know, to release her, so she can go away and be happy or something."

"You've been watching way too much TV. Remember, there are a lot more stories about people having the flesh ripped off their bones or vampires coming out of basements to bite you so you become a zombie for the rest of your life, not to mention snakes and spiders that might come pouring out of all those holes in the walls.

"Let's get serious here—we are not staying in that house!"

———

The tall canyon walls hid the morning sun until about seven o'clock, when it finally shed light on two humps on the riverbank.

Only with the coming of the dawn did the two humps actually fall asleep. All night long, Mogi never took his eyes off the windows, waiting and wondering, while Jennifer sat up, not using the lantern but counting on moonlight to reveal anything creeping toward them. They both half expected a woman to come dancing through their campsite at any moment.

Only one strange thing had occurred during the

night, but neither knew if it meant anything. They heard a swoosh. A big swoosh, the way it sounds when a big bird passes close overhead, not beating its wings but gliding.

It made them both sit up and look into the sky.

"What in the world was that?" Jennifer had asked.

The moon had passed behind the canyon walls and nothing but starlight held out against the darkness. They continued to look and listen, wondering if ghosts made swooshing sounds, and then lay back in their sleeping bags in silence. Only in the earliest dawn did they fall asleep.

It didn't take long for the morning sun to heat their sleeping bags to somewhere close to boiling, which woke them both up in an exhausted sweat. Struggling back into the house to find shade, they were dozing when the sound of meshing gears echoed down the canyon.

In the largest four-wheel drive, four-door, long-bed diesel pickup the ranch owned, Bud and Granddad drove slowly around the mounds of debris on the road. Pulling up in front, they stood and surveyed the house as the younger Franklins yawned, stretched, and shook themselves out.

"Must've been a helluva night," Bud said as he looked the two over.

Mogi looked at him through bleary eyes. "Let's just say we were very happy to see the sun come up." He opened the cardboard box and attacked a sandwich.

"You see any more ghosts?" Granddad asked.

"We've had enough close encounters for a lifetime," Jennifer said. "Right now, I just want to get out of this place."

"Why don't you get your stuff into the pickup while I take a little tour," Granddad said. "I haven't had the privilege of meeting your lady friend yet."

"She's upstairs, second bedroom on the left, unless she's in the fourth bedroom on the right," Mogi said, licking his fingers. Thinking this might be his last visit to Mulvaney Castle, he hurried after Granddad, sandwich in hand.

Standing in one of the downstairs rooms, Bud laughed at the holes in the wall and the hoof marks along the floor.

"Boy, they did a number on the place, didn't they! Good thing you guys got out of the way. That's what you do with horses—always assume they know more than you do. If somethin' goes wrong, just let 'em go and get out of the way."

Granddad was interested in the wallpaper and closely inspected the woodwork in each of the rooms, as well as the details around the stairwells. He was in no hurry.

Mogi showed him how to step up the stairway to get to the second story.

"This is really some house," he kept saying.

Mogi led everyone up the closet stairway and through the attic rooms. He told about the eyebrow window and how he had measured everything but couldn't find it from the inside.

"Could be just a roof vent, I suppose," Granddad said. "But that wouldn't explain the glass and the lace. I'd like to see it from the outside."

———

Back downstairs, Jennifer and Bud took the supplies to the pickup while Mogi walked his grandfather around to the side of the house. They spent several minutes discussing the window. Resigning themselves to the mystery, they joined the other two in the truck.

"I swear," Bud said as he guided the pickup through the ruts in the road leading out of the canyon, "lightning, thunder, hail, flashflood, ghosts— you had everything but Comanches riding down on you."

"Hey," Mogi remembered, "did you eat the calf's head?"

Bud and Granddad erupted in laughter, having enjoyed the novelties of the night before.

"I tell you what," Bud responded, "you two missed a pretty unique event. Let me first say, those ol' cowboys were a tough bunch. If they thought a calf's head was good eatin', then you have to remember that they sometimes were so starved they ate the leather of their boots. I did, indeed, have my share of calf's head, and rattlesnake stew, and slumgullion stew, and wild potatoes and onions mixed with fresh rabbit, and almost made it through a cup of coffee that was strong enough to remove paint."

"On the other hand," Granddad added, "the steaks were an inch thick and were to die for. They used cactus, dried tomatoes, and wild onions to make a salsa that beat anything I've ever eaten. And I've never tasted biscuits as good as the ones they made in the Dutch ovens. I may have to come up with something for Christmas that will celebrate the cowboy ways.

"I'll probably skip the calf's head, though."

CHAPTER 14

AUGUST 1877—SEVEN YEARS AFTER THE KIDNAPPING

There were the storms in the Palo Duro, then the land of many snows, then the time with Sitting Bull and his Sioux. Then the winter north of the Arkansas, and then back to Texas, where they wintered in the canyons of the Llano Estacado twice.

Six winters meant that he had been a Comanche for seven years.

Again this year, there was no party.

He was the tallest Indian in his village by a foot. He had never met a taller Indian. He was strong and broad-shouldered, his chest and arms sinewy with muscle. His hands and feet seemed as large as a grizzly bear's paws.

No one had ever seen a warrior like him, so lithe and athletic, so quick and deadly. He acted without fear, fought without reserve, and killed without regret. Everything about him was large: He had made a special bow that was half again the length of others, his arrows made to match, his tomahawk looked like an axe, his shield was the height of older children. He wore his hair in two braids down the side of his head, though he was known to unbraid it during battle to let it flow in the wind as a sign to his enemy.

Red Hair, giant of the Comanches, warrior of the chief. His enemies knew and feared him. On the plains, the ranchers and settlers watched over their shoulders to see if Red Hair was coming, the Army searched battlefields for arrows that could have belonged only to him, notices were sent out to towns telling of his sightings. His heart, they said, was a raging storm. His eyes, they said, were wild. Wild eyes that held no mercy.

Seven years.

Tip sat quietly on his horse as he watched the valley of teepees before him. He still sometimes woke in the night with visions of the big house, of his parents, and of Lucy, but the memories had grown dim and confused. His mind thought of fewer things now. He focused on water, food, shelter, protection, and war. Those things were demanded by today, and thoughts of yesterday were a luxury.

Times had changed. The land swarmed with white settlers like flies on a dead buffalo, and soldiers seemed to be everywhere. He led his warriors to attack, then flee, attack, and flee again. They were too few of them to fight extended battles. Even the battles they won were costly.

More often than not, he avoided battles, changing camps, moving his people, going deeper into where the white man did not want to go.

The Llano was the land no one wanted, with flat grass prairies and waterless reaches that kept people away. What was left of the Comanche lived along one river here, or one valley there, or in canyons and caves if they could find them, always moving, dodging, and hiding, hoping to avoid being discovered.

His chief, the father he loved, had died. Wrapped in a red blanket and placed on stones, a stick and grass shelter built over him, his horse and dog were killed and laid around him. The tribe wept, and then moved on.

The chief now dwelled in the spirit world.

The new chiefs were not like the old chief. They were tired of war and did not have the spirit to continue. They allowed the government agent to come and negotiate a treaty. Part of the treaty, as they had expected, was the return of all captives to the government.

Red Hair was a captive. Red Hair would be returned to the white man.

Tip protested over and over. He hated the whites. He had killed them, stolen their horses and mules, ravaged their possessions, burned their houses, eaten their animals.

They were not his people. He was not white.

He was Comanche.

But the new chiefs were jealous of the great warrior Red Hair and they wanted him gone.

When the government agent came to declare the treaty done, the tribe began the long, slow march to the reservation located in the Indian Territories, near Fort Sill.

Captives were taken a few miles farther and held at a school run by the Dutch church until they could be claimed by their families.

Red Hair refused and left the tribe. He and others fled into the wilds of the canyons, hiding for a long time. His was a lonely band of people—always chased, always tracked, always on the run. They grew tired, sick, and starved, and he knew they could not run forever.

One day, full of sorrow for the death of his people and expecting that his own death would be soon, he turned his horse toward the enemy and rode through the tall gates of Fort Sill. The gates slammed shut behind him.

Red Hair, the great Comanche warrior, slid down from his horse into a world as strange to him as the other side of the moon.

CHAPTER 15

PRESENT DAY

Bud knew it was bad when he saw the State Police cars.

It had taken until early Sunday afternoon to return to the ranch from rescuing Mogi and Jennifer at Mulvaney Castle, and he had been out of touch with the ranch since dawn. As they approached the turnoff from Highway 419, they saw the roadblock: Access to the Buffalo Skull Ranch was now limited to those only on official business.

Two hundred dead.

A hundred forty dead cattle had been found that morning close to the Canadian River, another thirty-eight along the northern boundaries in Camp Six, and another twenty-two a mile to the east along the cliffs. The dead cattle in the last two places were far from water. That fact alone made the situation more complicated and urgent—it meant that whatever was killing the animals was now traveling by air.

At headquarters, Mogi and Jennifer watched Bud and Granddad disappear into a crowd of inspectors, state officials, news reporters, ranch staffers, and hacienda guests who were milling around the front door. Within the hour, an official with the Livestock Board announced that the Buffalo Skull was closed for all animal-related business.

The hacienda and all dude ranch services could continue, but the cattle at the ranch were to be placed in pastures isolated from the horses and other farm animals. Ranch hands would be reduced to only those needed to maintain the stock, and only stored hay and well-water were to be used for feed.

The newly dead cattle were to be autopsied. If no clear evidence of the cause of death were found, it would be the state's decision that an invasive virus strain was attacking the herds, and all the cattle would be slaughtered as a precaution against an epidemic.

Three days would be allowed for the autopsies and analysis. At noon on Wednesday, the final decision would be made.

———

Jennifer was exhausted. She wished she could take a nap, but the hacienda was a busy place on Sunday afternoons.

The researchers had packed up and left after brunch.

The museum staff remained, joined by two more people who arrived at about noon. That afternoon's meeting was intended to be a planning session, but it drifted into a general discussion of what was happening at the ranch.

Jennifer knew her job. There were rooms to clean, rooms to refresh, new guests to be taken care of. Sunday supper would be a casual-dining affair, with leftovers from the night before served to those who might want a second helping of rattlesnake stew.

The leftover calf's head would not make a second appearance.

Mogi helped with the separation of the cattle. Each pasture had stock tanks that were filled by windmills, so it wasn't hard to get the herds isolated where they would have water. Large metal feed bins were hauled out and put close to the tanks. Tractors soon followed, picking up large rolls of hay from a trailer and sliding them into the bins. Hay would be the main feed source for the cattle.

Bud wanted to cancel all of the hacienda's activities but, after a long and intense conversation with Lassiter Jones, had decided to let the week go on as planned. He also realized he was going to need every penny he could get to manage the quarantine, so keeping the museum's money would help. All reservations after that were canceled.

Bud directed the cooks for the hacienda, the headquarters, and the outlying camps to avoid eating any meat, vegetables, or fruits produced at the ranch and to only use bottled water. The staff and ranch hands were asked to stop taking baths if their water wells were within five hundred feet of the Canadian River.

It was seven o'clock before Jennifer finally collapsed into a chair on the patio.

"Well, dear, the bright spot is that I've decided to stay for another week," Nedra Hamilton announced as she came over and sat down.

"Am I looking that bad?" Jennifer asked.

"You look like a first-year 4-H'er who's just figured out that her pet calf is going to end up on the table."

"Oh, Professor, everything is just so bad in so many ways!" Jennifer cried. "They're going to have to kill all the cattle, the ranch is going to be in ruins, Bud's going to lose his job, and there'll never be another chuckwagon supper at this great, old place again. It's just not fair!"

The older woman put her arm around Jennifer's shoulders.

"Let me tell you something. Being a historian is a curse. We deal every day, all day long, with stories that didn't happen to us. They always happened to someone else, and we didn't even know about it until months, years, or even centuries afterward.

"So we learn to approach life knowing that the action of one moment has never ended the future. If it had, we wouldn't be here. Will the cattle need to be killed? We've got a few days before that decision—wars have started and finished in less time. Will the ranch be forever condemned? Well, maybe what's poisoning the cattle will start an investigation that will save millions of cattle later on. The land will always be here, though what happens on it may change. And Bud's a survivor—he'll do fine. It may just be at something else from now on.

"I thought that my going to Mulvaney Castle would bring some kind of closure to the tragedies of the past—a father hung because of a reckless mistake, a mother who kills herself because there is no love left in the world, a son who's snatched to who knows what destiny, and an abandoned daughter who dies remembering a secret that we'll never understand.

"Is it fair? Who knows? I would have liked to find something in that house to explain the three words on the telegram and to believe that knowing the meaning of those three words would reveal a truth that could wrap up a lingering, frustrating story that's hung around in my family for a hundred and fifty years. Well, I didn't find it, and I guess my family will continue to live without ever knowing.

"We've laughed all week about all the crazy cowboys making lives out of loving horses and pushing cows, but we haven't stopped to count all the graves those cattle stepped on as they went north, nor the lives that were lost for what was really just another way to make money."

"Wow, you're really making me feel a lot better," Jennifer said through her tears.

The professor smiled. "Being a historian is a curse, but it's also a blessing. You learn that history rarely depends on you. You learn patience. It's like we're in a prizefight and we're fighting the other guy for all we're worth, and we keep waiting for the bell to ring and for the match to be over. Then, at some point down the line, we figure out the bell never rings."

CHAPTER 16

M ogi had never felt so bad. He came to be a cowboy and had tasted what it was like to be part of something that had a heritage—a way of living defined by good, smart, tough people who were in touch with soil and sky and wind and rain and sun and moon and water and grass and easy times and hard times. It was the kind of life that had been going on for hundreds of years, and he became part of it.

Extraordinary people, extraordinary times. All of them became a part of history, and some of them actually made history. He had stepped into that history and ridden freely, even if not very well. He now knew a little about cowboys and cowgirls who were real, with no makeup or Hollywood lights. They rode from dawn to dusk in every kind of weather, doctored cows and horses when needed, understood grass and water and weather, and were relaxed in knowing what, when, and how to do whatever it took to get their jobs done.

Now everyone was facing a mystery that they could not solve—and could not even identify—and he was just as dumbfounded as anybody. He was used to being one step ahead of those around him. He was used to seeing the answer when others couldn't even see the puzzle. But, like everyone else, he had no clue, no inkling of what was going on. When his time had come to pay everybody back for giving him such an extraordinary experience, he had failed.

He had failed Bud and Granddad, and he had failed Jennifer.

All the cowboy history of the Buffalo Skull Ranch was coming to an end. They'd kill the cattle, and the value of the ranch would plummet. The ranch owners would be bankrupt, Bud would lose his job, and everyone would be let go.

Somebody else would buy the ranch for pennies, and do what, raise cattle? No one would ever again trust the water or the soil. Start a dude ranch? No one would do that under the threat of possible disease. Leave the land alone? No one could afford that. A wind farm? Acres and acres of solar panels?

The end was coming to what had been a big part of history since Charlie Goodnight led the first steer through the shadows of the sandstone cliffs.

After leaving Bud and Granddad to face the crowds, Mogi roped a horse out of the corral, saddled up, and joined the others at Camp One, expecting to help push the cattle toward the watering tanks so they could be controlled. But he found that all the work was done. The camp bosses had gotten the hands lined out, driven the cattle, and had already designated the cowhands who would keep the stock compressed into their holding pens.

The remaining men and women had drifted on to headquarters or to their own homes.

That left him with nothing to do, so he turned and headed for the cliffs above the Canadian, hoping that maybe he'd get lost.

And so he sat, looking down at the river, thinking his thoughts of failure and frustration.

At least the ride had been good. The sun was high and the air was hot, but riding gave him a breeze that cooled his face beneath his hat, and he could feel small whiffs of air blowing between the buttons on his shirt. The recent rains had greened the landscape, releasing the scents of sagebrush and buffalo grass. The many-branched desert cacti were covered with yellow and orange flowers.

Watching the river helped to calm him, so Mogi decided to continue north. The trail would take him to Camp Six, but it would also allow him to get closer to the cliffs and the river and let him think even more about the strange house that had been both exciting and frightening. He would at least have those memories to add to his summer adventures.

Mogi felt the saddle beneath him and listened to the creak of the worn leather and the jingle produced by the bridle's metal rings. He had ridden enough this summer to feel comfortable, to blend with the movements of the horse, to move his body in the right motion. It was a satisfying feeling, one that gave him a quiet sense of pride.

He had become a cowboy, and that was something to be proud of, even if he couldn't save the ranch.

As he crested a small hill, he saw a solitary rider in the distance. He could see the man and the horse, but not much else. They were too far away. Still, there was something different about how the rider was sitting that Mogi couldn't quite figure out.

The rider held up a hand, made a kind of motion, and then turned and stepped his horse for a few strides. Then he looked back at Mogi.

Mogi couldn't figure it out.

The rider repeated the actions.

He wants me to follow him, Mogi finally decided. He had never met a single rider on the plains before. Usually, he came across groups of riders who were working—riding fence, looking for strays, moving cows from one place to another. If someone signaled, Mogi knew that help was being asked for.

Mogi turned his horse toward the man in the distance, gave more rein, leaned forward slightly, and lightly touched his spurs to the horse's flanks. The man turned and rode away, slowly at first but then at a fast lope. Mogi had to run his horse to keep up. It was surprising—usually, other riders waited for you to join them.

The country was rough but familiar. They were

headed for the S curve of the Canadian River. For pushing his horse as hard as he was, Mogi had not gotten any closer to the other horse and rider. He watched as they sailed over the ground ahead of him.

It suddenly occurred to Mogi why the way the man sat on his horse seemed different—he had no saddle. That was strange enough, but as the man drew close to the river, having slowed to follow the winding trail, Mogi had a clearer view.

The man had no clothes on.

Oh, yeah, it's a hot day, Mogi thought, but nobody goes naked on the back of a horse. It's gotta hurt!

Mogi shortened the gap between them before hitting the trail around the S curve and then topped a small hill before entering the canyon. The man was stopped in front of him, closer than before.

The man was actually not naked—he wore a breechclout and leggings that were a deep tan, like oiled leather, and which were hardly a different color from the man himself. In his hand he carried a spear and a shield, and when he turned to look at Mogi, his face was striped across the cheeks with different colors. His hair was long and red, hanging in two braids down his back.

Whoa.

Mogi was looking at an Indian. Not an Indian like today, but like from a hundred and fifty years ago. Cheesy Western movies had them made up like clowns, but Mogi had seen the paintings of Remington and Russell, and this man looked like he had just stepped out of one of their pictures.

But no painter had ever given an Indian red hair.

The man turned and his horse jumped to a gallop.

Mogi shivered in his saddle and spurred his horse on.

At the head of the S curve, the man turned left, not right. Turning right was the trail to Mulvaney Castle.

Going left was entering into the big canyon of the Sabinoso Wilderness that Mogi had seen when looking at Hector Valdez's map. It was a large tract of land that had recently been designated a wilderness area. It had several canyons, the biggest one directly ahead of him.

Okay, Mogi thought, we go left.

Portions of the S curve were full of mud and weeds from the flashflood, but most of it had dried, and he had no trouble getting up to the start of the left-hand canyon.

The trail was not well traveled and not well suited to a horse, but the man kept pushing ahead, and Mogi followed as best he could.

Up, up, then to a side canyon, then up more, threading their way among boulders, outcroppings, and juniper trees. The trail was now not much more than a faint path.

The Indian knew the way, still distant enough that Mogi would not even consider shouting at the man.

Mogi couldn't follow at the same speed and would lose sight of the man, and then he would finish a section of the trail and find the man ahead, waiting.

We're going all the way up, that's for sure, Mogi thought, but I have no idea why.

Around two more curves and through a barely visible opening in an oak thicket, Mogi rode over a rocky ridge into a patchy forest of pine trees.

He was on top of the mesa that made the west boundary of the large canyon. While riding, he had focused only on what was in front of him, but now he looked out across the breadth of the wilderness. It consumed the horizon.

He brought the horse to a walk, letting him rest from the effort of the last few minutes, and looked for the man who had brought him here. There was no one ahead of him. The Indian on the horse was gone.

The patch of trees gave way to a wide meadow, flat and free of sagebrush and small trees. Mogi looked for horse tracks but could see nothing but random tire tracks.

Tire tracks?

Bringing his horse to a halt, Mogi stood up in his saddle and turned all the way around, looking slowly and carefully around the meadow and into the scattered piñon and ponderosa pine around the edges, across occasional clumps of oak bushes.

He sat and thought about it and realized he had to have been following a ghost. The Indian's horse had left no tracks! He'd never before let himself believe in ghosts—that was irrational—and now he'd seen two? He felt confused and disoriented. Another shiver ran down his spine and he felt the hair on the back of his neck stand up.

But here is where he was meant to come, and this

is what he was meant to see, and in his heart, he knew he wasn't going to see the Indian anymore. Just like the woman in the white dress wasn't going to be in the window anymore.

CHAPTER 17

Supper was over and cleaned up by the time Mogi made it back to the barn, brushed down his horse, and changed. He talked Jennifer into stealing some cake and asked Granddad to join them as they drew their chairs together next to the glowing embers of the patio fire, where he told them what had happened.

"I went back to where the trail topped the ridge and walked my horse back and forth across the meadow, looking for anything unusual," Mogi explained. "I never found any horse tracks but my own, but I found a lot of other tracks. Look at these."

Mogi swiped to the pictures on his phone of a large area where grass had been trampled down and ruts had been left in the dirt. Different pictures showed boot tracks, motorcycle-like tire tracks, and big truck-tire tracks. He had several pictures of three motorcycle tracks side by side, where three riders had clearly ridden together.

"This is what the Indian wanted me to see. He led me there, so they've got something to do with everything that's going on."

Granddad looked closely at each photo, agreeing with Mogi as to what they showed, but not certain what they meant.

"Well, there's probably a lot of ground up there that's been worked over by hunters, or maybe groups out riding their ATVs. I'm not sure this isn't just another piece of information that doesn't help a lot."

A pain of rejection went through Mogi. It had been no dream, the man had led him there for a reason. "But the Indian was not a mirage—I didn't dream him up. And the lady in the window wasn't my imagination, either. They've got something to do with solving the mystery of the cattle deaths, and what we have to do is figure it out."

"I'm not saying that anything hasn't happened, or that there isn't a purpose to it happening, or that we don't need to figure out what it means. This is the Southwest," Granddad said with a small smile, "and we know that strange things happen in the Southwest on a regular basis. But the sum total of what we know and what we can do about it doesn't seem to have changed much. If the two of you say you saw a woman in a window, then I believe you, but that doesn't make it reasonable to anyone else.

"It looks like it's out of our hands, anyway. I think ol' Bud has given up. He left this afternoon for Santa Fe to talk to the Livestock Board members. He's not sure the ranch has any options left, but he's staying over through Tuesday to possibly see the governor.

"I'm leaving early in the morning to join him. Maybe I can lend some support for at least putting off the decision for a while."

———————

After Granddad went to bed, Jennifer tried to soothe Mogi. "He's not saying that he doesn't believe you," she said.

"But he doesn't believe me! He doesn't believe you either. You saw the woman at the castle. Do you think you imagined it?"

"No, I didn't imagine it. And I believe that an Old West Indian led you to the mesa top. I believe it but I don't understand it, and I am really spooked because we seem to be in the middle of all kinds of unbelievable stuff. But you have to remember that Granddad and Bud haven't seen the woman or the Indian. What they're focused on is facts they can take to the Livestock Board, and describing encounters with ghosts—especially ones they haven't personally seen—would probably not go over very well. They have to stick with the facts they have, and what they have is just not much."

"Well, that's fine for them and that's fine for you, if you think that you've done all you can, but it's not fine with me!"

Mogi stormed away.

———

The next day was bad all the way around.

It was Monday. With Bud gone, Mogi helped out in the barn, but several ranch hands were standing around with nothing to do, so any real work to be done was quickly taken care of or just ignored. Without Granddad to talk to and with Jennifer busy with her work, he sulked the day away.

Supper was a little better, visiting with Jennifer and Professor Hamilton. The professor had a new selection of stories about the Old West, but she could tell her audience wasn't up for entertainment. They parted early.

After supper, he walked around the headquarters a few times and then stopped to listen to the buzz of the guests discussing the activities the museum might host as part of the cattle drive exhibits.

He finally found himself sitting in the empty bunkhouse, disgusted. The other cowboys had gone out to the different camps, where they could at least do nothing without being watched, so he found himself alone, listening to the noises outside. He finally went to bed.

He was still listening an hour later.

Giving up on sleep, he pulled on his jeans and shirt, sat at the desk under the window, and put his head in his hands. He was tired and wrung out, but his mind felt caught in the center of a hundred bumper cars—he kept trying to go forward but kept getting hit in other directions.

How do you kill thousands of cows? Shoot them? Poison them? Bleed them?

How do you justify killing the three hundred new calves they had branded in June?

What do you do with them after they're dead? Bury them? Burn them? Just let them lie around and rot? Do you have to keep blood samples, hair samples, or hides?

How deep do you have to bury a cow? Does the ground cave in when the body rots?

It was depressing, and he felt his mind spinning out of control.

The problem was slowing down enough so he could think about things one at a time. He could remember a lot, but there was nothing that told him what was important and what wasn't.

Taking some paper from the desk drawer, Mogi made a list:

1. The cattle began dying in July. Small groups at first, but the last group—Sunday morning—was big.

2. Most of the cattle died close to the river, but the last groups—Sunday morning—were a mile or more away, some even close to the cliffs. Does that mean that it isn't the water?

3. There's no explanation for the deaths. Virus? Bad water? Bad guys? Accidental or deliberate? How do you kill a cow without leaving a trace?

4. The ghost woman has appeared to me twice, to Jennifer once. Why would she appear? Does her appearance have anything to do with the cattle, or is it something else?

5. Nedra Hamilton is the great-granddaughter of Lucy

Mulvaney. Lucy was the kidnapped boy's sister, she was six at the time of the kidnapping.

6. Why did Nedra collapse? Does the castle have a spirit?

7. "Run Lucy run" means what? What does Lucy running have to do with anything? Run where? Run from someone? Run to someone?

8. An Old West Indian appeared to me, it certainly had to be another ghost. Why? What purpose did the appearance serve? Was he leading me to the answer of the cattle deaths? Could it have been a regular person just dressed up? To fool me? What for?

9. The clearing had a lot of people and vehicle tracks. So what?

10. The Indian's horse left no tracks.

11. The little window in the castle—where is it? Why was it built in the first place? Why can't I find it?

He listed more things, wrote notes in the margins, reread what he had written, marked through words, changed others, and then sat and stared at what he had written. Granddad was right: There wasn't a lot to even talk about, much less make an argument with. Nobody was going to listen to stories about a ghostly woman and a mysterious man dressed like an Indian.

He pulled out his phone and swiped through his pictures from the day he had arrived. The hacienda, the headquarters buildings, horses, cattle, other ranch hands, the cowboy band, the chuckwagon, the castle, the junction of the two rivers, the prairies, a few sunsets, the latest pictures from the top of the mesa, including the meadow, the ridge, the trampled grass, and the tracks in the dirt.

The tracks.

Mogi enlarged the pictures he had taken on top of the mesa and looked closely at the three side-by-side motorcycle tracks. It couldn't be motorcycles, he decided, unless three people could ride perfectly alongside each other, which didn't make any sense. They used to make three-wheeled ATVs, he remembered, but the tracks weren't big enough for ATV tires, and the three-wheelers hadn't been made for years anyway.

What else has three wheels?

An airplane has three wheels.

Nope, couldn't be that. The meadow wasn't long enough—it takes a long runway to get a plane off the ground, and that meadow probably wasn't smooth enough. Landing it would be impossible, unless it was a bush plane like in Alaska, which can use tiny runways.

Mogi closed his eyes, trying to think, trying to organize the bits of information into some pattern that would make sense. He yawned. His head was filled with ideas, but closing his eyes left him without the distraction of sight and his head began to slowly droop, nodding closer and closer to the desk. Finally, his forehead touched and Mogi yielded up to all the weariness that the last two days had brought.

He slept, but his mind kept going.

He was on the porch at the castle. Not the broken-down porch that was a heap of splintered parts, but a beautiful porch, bright with paint, the floorboards shiny in the light streaming out the window, past the fine lace curtains. The view inside was vibrant, with people talking and singing, the piano playing loudly while others danced happily around and around the rooms. The rooms appeared larger than what he knew they were, the light from the many lanterns inside giving life to the walls that, days earlier, had been old, worn, and dark. The woman in the white dress was there, swinging with a bright smile as she danced with a man, a large man with a carefully combed head of red hair. Children ran in and out of the rooms playing, and it was easy to pick out the daughter and son. Six years old, ten years old, red hair.

Suddenly, the song was over and the children were gone.

There was yelling and screaming, and people ran outside, watching in the sky as Indians, dressed like the man on the horse but riding on the backs of eagles, swooped down and stole the boy, all the while laughing and chanting their tribal songs, pointing at the dead cows that lay all over the yard and in the river. The little girl was running, running, running, hurrying down the road, crying, calling for the boy to come back. The people cursed loudly at the sky, at the eagles, at the house, at the injustice of things being taken by thieves in the night. The Indians kept laughing, swooping down at the people, shooting arrows at them, swooping and making them fall to the ground frightened.

Tears made little rivers in the dirt.

The woman in the white dress stood in the window, her hand raised in a sorrowful goodbye.

Mogi woke up. Beads of sweat had dripped onto the desk. He opened his eyes, rubbed them, and took a deep breath. He now knew what had made the tracks in the dirt and how the killing of the cattle was done. He didn't know why or the exact method of bringing death, and he certainly didn't know who was doing it.

He needed to set a trap, and he didn't have much time to do it.

He picked up the pencil and added to his list: *There was a big swoosh in the middle of the night.*

CHAPTER 18

"Are you going to do something dangerous?" Jennifer asked, looking her brother in the eye.

"Absolutely not. I'm just going to take pictures."

"Why don't we wait until Granddad and Bud get back? It shouldn't be too long."

Mogi looked around the room in frustration.

"Listen, do you think they're going to believe me? Do you think they'd listen to the theory of a fourteen-year-old dork after talking with the governor? Besides, we don't have time. This is Tuesday, and the Livestock Board makes their decision tomorrow. Tonight is the only night for us to force whoever's been killing the cattle to try it one more time.

"I've got to be in that clearing tonight. I can't take a horse because I can't come down in the dark on horseback, I'd kill us both. So I'll ride to the S curve, send the horse back, hike up to the clearing, which is going to take a couple of hours, wait until something happens, get the pictures, and then I'll meet you at the castle as soon as I can get over there."

"But are you sure that whoever it is is going to show up?"

Mogi gently touched her arm. "If you'll spread the story, I am absolutely sure that whoever is behind this will make one last killing before the Livestock Board meets. They'll have to. They can't risk the Board not shutting the ranch down when they're this close."

"Do you think people are actually going to believe that it was a bee?"

"A *swarm* of bees. Make sure you tell everybody that the inspectors are convinced that it was a *swarm* of bees. Killer bees, carrying some sort of African poison that gives the cows paralysis of the lungs or something. You don't have to go into detail. Just let everybody know that you heard from Bud and this is what the officials are believing, and that it was a fluke migration of the bees that they believe has ended. They believe the bees have left the area and the ranch won't have to be closed or the cattle destroyed."

Jennifer didn't look convinced. "I want it on the record that I'm not sure this is going to work. If you spend all night up there for nothing, then you've earned it."

"Well, maybe so. But I've got to try. Will you do it? And meet me at the castle in the morning?"

Jennifer nodded.

CHAPTER 19

I t was so far into Tuesday night that it must have been Wednesday morning, and Mogi was getting really, really sleepy. The only thing keeping him awake was his periodic sneezing from being surrounded by juniper trees. Their scent tortured his sinus passages, but the trees hid him from the meadow, a hundred feet from the opening in the oak bushes at the rim of the canyon, right where the Indian ghost had led him.

At about three o'clock, the distant sounds of a diesel engine broke the monotonous quiet. Headlights appeared, bouncing up and down as a pickup with a covered trailer negotiated the rough ground into the meadow.

Jerking over the ruts, the pickup jostled back and forth as it positioned the trailer.

Mogi looked through his binoculars. The quarter moon provided just enough light to see what was going on.

His jaw dropped.

The pickup was huge, dual-wheeled, with running lights front to back, large exhaust pipes running up the sides of the cab, and big University of Oklahoma decals on the doors.

It was Lassiter Jones!

Mogi couldn't believe it. How was Dr. Jones mixed up in this? Why?

He watched as the rotund man crawled from the cab, walked to the trailer, let down the ramp door, and went inside. In a few moments, a large contraption of sorts—a frame on three wheels—slid down the ramp and onto the grass. Mogi could see a motor and a large propeller with a seat behind the front wheel.

Lassiter Jones pushed it forward a few yards, straightened it so that the front wheel pointed across the clearing, and then went back inside the trailer. He came back with a bundle of long pipes that he hooked to the contraption and then spread apart. The pipes had cloth between them. Once open, the pipes and cloth became a big, triangular wing.

Mogi smiled. His guess had been right on the money.

The contraption was a motor-driven glider, an ultralight—a light, strong single-seat aircraft that could be easily handled by one person.

Lassiter went back inside the trailer and then reappeared with two small gas cylinders that he attached along the bottom of the back frame.

The Sabinoso Wilderness, a newly declared wilderness area, was still closed to the public. That meant that several square miles of wilderness had absolutely no one in it. Absolutely no one to hear strange noises at night, and absolutely no one to notice somebody flying around in the dark.

The engine and propeller would get the glider off the ground and high into the sky. Turning the motor off, the glider was light enough to ride the strong wind currents coming up the face of the cliffs.

Just like the birds.

At will, the glider could swoop down into ranch property. The pilot could select parts of the herd, quietly glide over them, release the gas from the cylinders attached to the frame, and then get the glider back to altitude. Once he had made his passes, the pilot could catch the wind and guide it back to the clearing in the wilderness. If the air currents weren't enough to get him there, the pilot could restart the motor.

Mogi had no idea what the chemical was or why it couldn't be detected after it had killed its target, but it had to be a gas, that was the only thing that fit. Until the last time, dead cattle had been found close to the river.

But the latest find of dead cows away from the river meant that the *disease* had been carried by air currents, necessitating a far quicker and more substantial response from the Livestock Board. That's why the ranch was quarantined so quickly.

Instantly, Mogi realized that on its last flight, on Saturday night, once it had released its gas far away east of the river, the glider caught the currents along the cliffs, went up and over the mesa, and took the shortcut through the Canadian River canyon to get back to the clearing. Having gone in that direction, it made a big swooshing sound as it passed over two half-awake people who had been up all night expecting a ghost.

Still, Lassiter Jones was behind this? It didn't make any sense. He was one of the good guys.

Mogi had to understand.

Making his way quickly across the clearing in the dark, he stopped about twenty feet away and used his phone to take a picture of the whole apparatus. The flash lit up the surrounding forest like a bomb.

"What the…"

"Dr. Jones!" Mogi called out. "What are you doing?"

The man's eyes were wide with surprise, and maybe fear.

He hit a switch that turned on lights around the trailer.

"Who…what…wait a minute. You're one of the ranch hands from the Buffalo Skull, aren't you?"

"What are you doing?" Mogi took another picture as he had moved sideways in the grass. This one would have the pickup. There was no mistaking the pickup.

Jones backed away from the machine, glanced around, and then relaxed and smiled. "Uh oh, looks like I've been caught. Wait a minute. Somebody made up the story about the bees, didn't they?"

"I knew whoever was killing cattle would make

another run if there was any chance that the Livestock Board wasn't going to shut the ranch down. But why you? I don't understand."

The man hesitated and then drew himself up to full height. "That ranch down there is where Goodnight was," he replied. "He rode that land, drove cattle, built campfires, looked at the stars. It was there that he became famous, there that he made history!

"Nobody else knows, but the owners were planning to sell the ranch. Getting out of the cattle business and going into investment banking or some other nonsense. But they wanted a hundred million dollars for it. A hundred million!

"I don't have a hundred million!" Jones said in a pleading voice. "I thought about selling my collections, making some other deals, bringing in some partners, but I could only put together fifty million, at most. I offered that last year, and they didn't even take me seriously. So I needed to get their price down. Don't you see what's at stake?

"I attended a talk some years ago about insects in the Amazon. There's a spider there whose poisonous bite is a thousand times the potency of cobra venom. It causes the heart of its victims to beat so fast that the heart outruns the blood and the animal dies. After a few minutes, the poison breaks down and is absorbed completely. All I had to do was make it into a gas and figure out a way to get it into the air."

The man shrugged and looked as if he had no choice. "Look, kid, a few more days and it'll all be over. It's just a bunch of cows."

"But why?" Mogi asked. "If they shut down the ranch, you wouldn't be able to raise cattle on it."

Lassiter Jones's face actually lit up in the pale moonlight. "Well, technically, you wouldn't be able to raise cattle if you intended to sell them," he said excitedly. "Listen, people have short memories. After a while, you could bring grazing back, but not for cattle. Five hundred thousand acres! What would you give to see a buffalo herd again? How about five hundred buffalo? How about five *thousand* buffalo? Completely free, running wild as far as they could run!

"What a sight that would be, watching a herd of those magnificent beasts thundering across the grass! No fences, no roads, no telephone wires. Or how about a thousand Texas Longhorns? Not the cross-breeds you see in pictures, but real, purebred, tough, huge, speckled Longhorn cattle with horns six, eight, ten feet across. Imagine driving a herd of those!

"And *real* cowboys, not the cheap rodeo imitations of today. Buffalo, Longhorns, cattle drives, chuck-wagon feasts. I bet ranches all around here would join in. We could end up with a million acres dedicated to celebrating the cowboy life. There'd be shops and restaurants and places for people to stay. And research facilities, breeding programs, genome mapping to get back the original breeds.

"In the last hundred and fifty years, we've ruined the natural state of this land. Thousands of buffalo would bring it back. They'd be all over, and it would be their hooves pounding into the ground that would make the grasses grow—grasses taller than you! We'd bring it all back—the animals, the grasslands, the natural stream flows, the long prairies with nothing on them except life—raw, original life! People could see the Old West as it really was. I'd make it happen! I'd be this generation's Charlie Goodnight! And you, my boy, you'd be my partner. We would be creating history, not just watching it go by. What do you say?"

Mogi was enthralled. The man wasn't evil—in fact, he was describing some of the things that Mogi himself had been dreaming about. It could be possible. Why not? All of the feelings about heritage that he had felt in such a small way—maybe other people could feel it, too. What would it feel like to be on a horse running flat out next to a stampeding buffalo herd?

Wait a minute, Mogi thought. Who are you kidding?

He flashed a picture with Jones leaning his foot up against the middle tire of the ultralight, with a smile no less, and then took off as fast as he could for the trail.

"Wait...you can't go...you're going to ruin everything!" Jones's voice trailed into the distance.

There was the bush, and, hoping he was lined up right, Mogi leaped through the open space. He hit the trail but fell back on the impact. Holding himself upright, he slid for a few feet as he felt pains shoot up his back. Getting his feet squared up beneath him, he stood up and began taking large steps as the rocks and dirt cascaded down the trail in front of him.

It was one thing to climb up a faint, steep trail in daylight, but going down in the dark, even with his flashlight, felt like he was stepping into space every time his boots went in front of him. His heart crawled into his throat as sweat slid down his face.

Dr. Jones had not sounded crazy, but the facts were plain: He was responsible for the deaths of several hundred cattle. He was willing to destroy a hundred more animals to get his own personal dream and, Mogi was sure, would ruin people's lives, as well.

If he were caught now, everything he had would be threatened—his personal life, his position at the museum, his financial standing—which meant that this was no longer a friendly conversation about cowboys and heritage. The man behind him had bet everything on not being discovered and would risk everything to make sure Mogi didn't make it back to the ranch with those pictures.

Behind him, he heard the motor start on the ultralight.

An acceleration, a long whine, and the glider took off into the air above him, looking like a vulture in the dark.

Mogi straightened up and concentrated on maintaining long strides rather than trying to run. It seemed like forever, but he finally reached the bottom of the canyon, where the smells of vegetation engulfed him. The trail was more open and easier to see here. Another few hundred yards and he'd be to the S curve, and then it would be only a mile more to the castle and Jennifer.

Swoosh! Whack!

Mogi fell forward, hitting the dirt with his shoulder and face, sprawling out across the trail. Dazed, he rolled over on his back, tried to get up, but fell back down. Now a lot more than his back was hurting.

Jones had turned off the engine and was riding the air currents, which made his movements silent. And deadly.

Mogi had just been hit by one of the wheels. What chance did he have if Jones decided to gas him?

Suddenly, the idea of waiting for Granddad and Bud didn't seem so bad.

Wobbling back onto his feet, Mogi stumbled forward to find his flashlight and staggered on down the trail. He had to be close to the river. Far above him, he heard the glider engine turn back on. Jones was gaining altitude for another run.

Letting his long legs fly, Mogi ran out of the canyon, made his way through the mud of the S curve, struggled in the soft sand of the canyon floor, and then lurched out of the riverbed and up the trail.

His only chance was to get to the castle and find Jennifer.

CHAPTER 20

Kneeling inside the house beneath a window, Mogi peeked over the sill to watch the glider touch down on the flat of the front yard. He struggled against the heaving of his chest, trying to slow the gasping for air and the pounding of his heart. He was sure he sounded like a bellows to anyone within a hundred feet.

But there wasn't anyone within a hundred feet. In particular, there was no Jennifer within a hundred feet. There had been no vehicle at the old house. Nothing. Nobody.

Then he realized that it was still before dawn, so Jennifer might not come for another hour.

That was a problem.

Mogi hadn't planned on needing a place to hide. He was expecting to jump into the pickup that Jennifer would have driven to the house, and Jones would then be out of luck. As the pickup climbed out of the canyons and along the road to town, there'd be no upward winds to help Jones chase them down, and he'd surely run out of gas.

Now what was he going to do?

Outside, the glider rolled to a stop. Dr. Lassiter Jones unbuckled his harness, stood up from the seat, and removed his helmet. He looked the house over for a minute and then reached into a bag hanging from the glider's frame. Carefully, deliberately, he strapped a pair of spurs to his boots, reached again into the bag, and carefully, deliberately, fit a two-pistol holster around his waist.

Mogi was sweating. What to do? Where to go? It was a big house. He could go up one stairway and down the other, or maybe out the back and try to run for the river. He could try hiding under some of the fallen porch, but if found, he'd be trapped.

Jones started across the yard.

There was no more time for Mogi to think. He had to do something. He had to hide. But where?

———

Jones was in no hurry, picking his way through the rubble of the porch. The light of the quarter moon had been enough to see the young man running along the riverbed and then sprinting toward the old house. He had made a tight turn for the landing and watched as Mogi ran through the front door.

Walking up the ramp, Jones stepped through the doorway and swept his flashlight around the rooms.

He'd always heard of this place but had never come to see it. It was a mess.

"You know, I almost pulled it off," Jones said loudly as if he were carrying on a conversation. "Took my time, read the newspapers on the Web every day, watched how the stories developed, felt the fear that grew over the weeks. Every few days or so, I'd come out, make a flight, and kill a few cows here and there, always close to the river, making it seem that the river was the problem. Now, son, you have to remember—I only killed cows. Who cares about cows when we're talking about building a ranch that would bring back so much that we've lost!

"I was right, though. It only took some cows to die for the price of the ranch to drop like a stone in water."

Jones's spurs made a light tinkling sound as he stepped lightly through the living room, around the chimney, and into the kitchen, holding the flashlight in front of him, stopping, watching, listening. He knew that the shadows would hide a lot, but he also knew that the young man must be breathing hard. And cowboy boots on a wood floor could hardly be quiet.

"But government moves slowly, doesn't it?" he continued. "The inspectors couldn't make up their minds, couldn't make a decision. Having contaminated water is a great fear, but things didn't seem to be going anywhere.

"Not fast enough, anyway. So I had to make it look

like it was in the air. An airborne virus is a much worse threat than bad water."

Jones circled into every room and then gingerly picked his way up the stairs toward the bedrooms. He checked the hall closet and saw the stairway to the attic. He stood silent for a moment, listening for any sound above him.

"I wish you'd come out!" he called. "I'm going to find you anyway, so you might as well get it over with."

Jones searched the attic rooms quickly and went back to the first floor. He stood and listened.

A dull thudding sound echoed from up the canyon. In a minute or two, growing in intensity, a diesel pickup from the ranch pulled up so that the glider was fully revealed in its headlights. Two people got out of the cab.

"Well, well, well. Looks like we have company," Jones said quietly. "That makes things a little difficult, but, ah, I believe I have a solution. Not one that I want, but it is what it is. I can't afford to lose now."

Tiptoeing across the floor as quietly as possible, he slipped out the back doorway and down the ramp that Mogi had made for the horses.

Closing the pickup door behind her and walking over to the ultralight, Jennifer ran her hand over part of the glider's wing, amazed again at her brother's gift for guessing the unknown.

Turning to her partner, she said, "Are you sure you're up to this?"

The other person nodded. "I'll just hang around. You go find your brother."

As silently as possible, Jennifer switched on her flashlight and moved slowly up the ramp and through the front door.

Even though sunlight was slowly creeping into the valley, a distant shadow went unnoticed as it passed along the outskirts of the yard, slipped along the riverbank, and came up behind the glider.

Jones undid one of the gas canisters from its holder.

Reaching up to get a respirator mask, he was already congratulating himself on finding a simple way to put his plan back on track. Three innocent visitors to a local landmark die from the same mysterious airborne virus that killed the cattle? It would be devastating news, and then it wouldn't just be the Livestock Board who would be calling for shutting down the ranch—it'd be the whole state.

He might not need the whole fifty million.

Stealing up to the side of the house, he lifted the canister into an open doorway and pointed the nozzle toward the room. Five minutes worth of the gas would circulate enough poison throughout the house to do the job, he thought. He'd need just a few minutes to get the glider up the river to a grassy area where it wouldn't leave tracks. He'd—

A loosely knotted lariat dropped over his head and shoulders.

"What the—" he yelled as he was jerked off his feet, rolled over, twisted around, and hogtied.

"Lassiter, you're an idiot!" a woman's voice said as a cane pressed against his neck and his guns were taken out of the holsters.

"Nedra! Oh, Nedra, thank God you're here! You can help me. I've told you about what it would be like to bring back an Old West ranch. This is our opportunity! The Buffalo Skull could be everything I imagined. You've got to tell them about the ranch we could make! Convince them that we could be making history, Nedra!"

Nedra Hamilton gave a snort. "Lassiter, shut up. You've got too many words for my ears."

Jennifer had watched it all from inside. Now she needed to find her brother. "Mogi! Where are you? Mogi!"

She flashed her light onto the walls as she ran through the rooms, stepping around the clumps of wood and plaster. A light bounced through the kitchen doorway and Mogi slowly appeared, walking stiffly toward her.

She grabbed him and held him tight as he straightened up, dust falling from his shoulders.

"You have no idea how glad I am to see you," she said.

CHAPTER 21

I t was mid-morning when the State Police helicopter took off with their prisoner. A hazmat team had arrived and taken away the canisters of gas. The local sheriff and his deputy were detailed to retrieve Jones's pickup, trailer, and glider.

Bud and Granddad had pulled up not long after Jennifer, having gotten the note she'd left telling them of Mogi's theory and his plans for the night.

"I do love my grandkids," Granddad said to Bud, "but that boy and I are going to have to have a talk about risk management. His mother is going to skin me alive when she hears what he did this time."

Finally, after the sheriff and the State Police and the FBI and the ranch people had come and gone, the five people who were left sat yawning against the stone foundation of the great house.

"Okay, it's time," Jennifer said in a definite voice. "Tell us what happened."

Mogi smiled slightly. He hadn't wanted to reveal

anything until the others had left. "Okay, but you have to let me go step by step. And everybody's going to need their flashlights.

"After Dr. Jones chased me out of the canyon, I ran into the house and then watched him land the glider in the front yard. When he got out and put his guns on, I really got scared. It looked like I'd gotten myself backed into a corner. He knew I was in the house, and I couldn't get out of the house without him hearing me, so I needed to hide. Let me show you what I did."

Mogi led the way up the plank ramp and through the front doorway. Granddad helped Nedra along. She walked in with no fear.

"Remember how many bookcases there are? They're all over the place. In particular, they're on both levels and always right next to a fireplace or stove."

He led them to the kitchen. Pointing at the mostly demolished bookcase, the others could see horseshoe marks around the walls and floor, as well as the direct hit that the bookcase had taken. Peering through the broken boards in the back, they could see empty space.

"It was dark, but I didn't dare use my flashlight. I could still make out the light color of the plaster walls and the dark places where the horses had kicked the walls. I thought maybe there'd be a hollow place in the wall or something that I could get into, and then I saw what had been done to the bookcase.

"Since it was built into the chimney, I thought maybe there was a space behind it and I could use boards to hide behind. So, while Jones was picking his way up the front, I pushed the broken boards out of the way and crawled in. While he was upstairs, I turned my flashlight on and looked around. There were hinges on the inside of the bookcase. That didn't make any sense until I shined the light into the chimney itself. And, what do you know—Martin Mulvaney hadn't just built the chimney to accommodate the fireplaces, he had also built it as a place to hide. These bookcases act as secret doors.

"If there was an Indian attack, anybody in the house who was close to a bookcase could push it open, get inside, and push it closed. The Indians would never have found them. Shining my light around, I then found something else that I would never have dreamed of. That's when Jennifer pulled up in the truck."

He kicked the remaining boards off the opening of the bookcase to make it big enough for everyone to bend over and walk through. On the inside, clouds of dust hung in the air, but he could see well enough to squirm past the piping and stand up. Shining his light above him, he could see several chimney pipes coming through the chimney's brick wall in several places.

Mogi used his hand to brush away enough dust to reveal a series of steep, narrow wooden steps, hardly enough tread to get a foot on, built into the sides of the chimney.

Keeping his flashlight pointed at his feet, he steadied himself with a hand against the brick as he tested each step. It felt firm, but sharp squeaks came from the boards as he stepped on them, one foot after the other.

Granddad followed, going ahead of Nedra and holding her hand as she confidently negotiated the steps. Jennifer followed closely, thinking she might have to catch the old woman, and then Bud. Bud had brought two flashlights from the pickup, and had given one to Jennifer. They were powerful enough to light up the whole inside of the chimney.

Winding his way up, stepping on landings that allowed other bookcases to open, moving his head and body around the various pipes, Mogi made steady progress upward through the chimney's insides.

At the top of the steps, he came to a small, narrow door, crowded between the bricks of the chimney before it went through the roof. Mogi reached carefully and gave the small doorknob a twist. It was difficult at first, but gave way after being jiggled. The door squeaked as it swung toward him and out of the way.

He gingerly stepped through the doorway as even more dust swirled up around him. He turned to help the others through the opening, and they all stepped down into a long room. In the ceiling of the room, which must have also been the inside of the roof, a tiny window, shaped like an eyebrow, complete with lace, let in a dim light from outside.

The room was stuffy, and a thick layer of dust lay over everything in sight, washing away all color. The room ran lengthwise with the roof, and the ceiling ran at an angle from the top of the inside wall to the opposite side of the floor. A number of rugs were scattered over the warped wood-floor slats.

On a writing table lay an oil lamp surrounded by stacks of books. A porcelain washbasin and pitcher sat on a short chest of drawers. Nearby was a rocking chair.

To the left of the door was a small pot-bellied stove, a box of kindling next to it. To the right side was a glass-paneled gun closet showing several rifles and pistols. Wallpaper covered the walls. A bed made of copper rods was set against the far end.

Unburnished, the copper had turned a dull black. What was left of the mattress, a thin layer of cotton bunting, was covered with quilts. Wire springs showed through the footboard.

But all eyes were riveted on what lay on top of the mattress.

Perhaps pure white when new, the dress was now yellowed, the satin dull in the glare of the flashlights. Fine layers of lace bordered the high collar, the bodice, and the sleeves, trailing down the long folds of the skirt to the ankles. The lace swirls were filled with drifts of soft brown dust.

That it was a wedding dress in decay, there was no doubt, but the skeleton it dressed still held a certain elegance. A sheer veil covered the face, but the pale skull could still be seen in contrast to the perfect white teeth.

What remained of any skin was thin and curled, baked from years of the hot, dry air of the Southwest.

Still framing her head, long strands of blond hair

swept from the pillow down across her shoulders. The bare bones of her hands still grasped the dry stalks of what must have been a small bouquet of flowers.

At the top of the bodice, as if placed over the heart, were two folded pieces of paper.

L U C Y was crudely written across the top of the first and appeared as only a piece of stationery. The second looked more formal, with thicker paper, folded and tied with a ribbon.

Mogi reached carefully to pick up the first paper, tapping it against his flashlight to shake off the dust. He handed it to Nedra.

She gently opened it under the lights where all could see.

L U C Y
W I R E G O O D N I G H T A T F O R T S I L L
I C O M E
T I P

"This is what the telegram meant," Nedra said quietly.

"This is where Lucy was supposed to run to. As a little girl, her parents would have taught her an emergency command, a phrase like, 'Run Lucy Run' that would be said if there was danger at the ranch. Hearing the phrase meant she was to go into the house, up the inside of the chimney, and into this room.

"So that's what her brother, Tip, told her to do. He sent her a telegram under the pretend name of Mr. Smith, and told her to come here, to this room, where she would find his note. She would have sent a telegram, and he would have come back to be united with her.

"Well, here I am, Tip," she said with a tear in her eye.

"A little late, but I finally made it."

CHAPTER 22

AUGUST 1878—EIGHT YEARS AFTER THE KIDNAPPING

A short, stocky man in a dust-covered, ill-fitting suit and narrow string tie rode his horse through the gated entrance of a compound about two miles outside of Fort Sill, Oklahoma. His face was deeply tanned around the eyes, and his Stetson hat was pulled down securely over a mop of stiff, graying hair. He wore a full beard, trimmed but straggly, as if the salt and pepper whiskers were trained to be unruly.

Pulling a saddled horse behind him, he fought the wind as he pulled up to a hitching post, dismounted, and tied both reins securely. Standing on the ground revealed why he seemed so short—his legs were so bowed that they had reduced his height by a couple of inches. Such was the result of riding a horse every day of his life.

Spitting a long stream of brown tobacco juice on the ground, he walked up the wooden steps of a building, crossed the porch, opened the door, and went inside.

"I'm Goodnight," he said in a rough voice. "I've come for the boy."

"Oh, yes, sir, Colonel. Let me get the superintendent," the clerk said as he rushed down a hallway.

The compound was a school for educating Indian children. Wichitas, Apaches, Kickapoos, Comanches, Arapahoes, Kiowas, Caddoes—there was a smattering of children from tribes across the plains and the Southwest, but most were from the Indian Territories of Oklahoma.

It was meant for their own good: preparation and training for a life that would no longer be in an Indian world, but in a new world they'd live in for the rest of their lives.

A white world.

The school also served as the gathering point for kidnapped children retrieved from the various tribes, children who had been taken, adopted into Indian families, or used as servants or slaves. Ranging in age from youngsters to almost adult, the captives were brought to the school, given baths, haircuts, and clothing, and then photographed. The photographs were circulated among towns and ranches where children had been taken or had gone missing. Parents, friends, and relatives would come, sort through the children, and try to remember.

Sometimes the children themselves remembered

their names, sometimes not. It was not unusual for them to have forgotten their birth language.

"You don't want him, Colonel," the superintendent said as they walked across the compound to a large dormitory. "He's too far gone, just a man-killing savage. We've had him almost a year and it hasn't made a spit's worth of difference. I would have let the Army hang 'im, but he's white, and the president's policy is clear about the whites. Your letter said you knew his family and were willing to take him. No one else has come, of course."

Goodnight spat, wiped his lips, and grunted.

The interview room was sparsely furnished with a table, a few chairs, and a corner table with a lamp. Framed maps of the territories and other documents hung on the walls. A picture of Rutherford B. Hayes was prominently displayed.

Goodnight sat down, squirming against the wood of the chair as the superintendent left the room. He was more comfortable sitting on the worn leather of a saddle.

A few minutes later, the superintendent returned. Following him was a figure that filled the doorway. The young man was huge, nearly seven feet tall, with broad shoulders covered by a too-small white shirt. He wore coveralls and moccasins.

His body was lean and well-muscled, his hands large and calloused. His hair, which had been cut with a pair of sheep shears, was a deep red. His skin was stretched like well-worn leather. Burn splotches highlighted the cheeks and forehead, evidence of a once light-skinned complexion. A large scar ran from his right ear up to his forehead.

Even though the features were that of a hard and tough life, he was clearly a young man. A teenager, maybe.

As the young man sat down, Goodnight watched his eyes flit around the room, across the two men, the table, the floor, the ceiling—an intense alertness, like an animal warily measuring his environment. An animal with wild eyes.

"Mr. Styrus, would you excuse us that we might talk privately?" Goodnight said.

The superintendent was openly nervous. He had expected to be asked to provide extra men as a safety precaution. As it was, he cautiously backed out of the room and indicated that he'd be right outside the door if needed.

Goodnight spat a stream of tobacco juice on the floor.

If the school was not courteous enough to provide a spittoon, it was not his problem. The man leaned forward onto the table and spoke clearly.

"I will be plain and talk straight. I'm Goodnight. I know who you are. I know what you've done. You and I have crossed paths three times, once up in Wyoming when you were winterin' with Sitting Bull, once when you hit my cattle in Colorado, and once on the Canadian, when you were stealin' my horses. Each time, you were set on takin' what was mine, and I was set on killin' you. I was unsuccessful.

"What your people did all over that land, from

north to south, even to Mexico, is open knowledge. You were called Red Hair for obvious reasons, and you led parties that killed men, women, and children with the same regard that I kill rabbits and snakes. I have killed, but I am not a savage.

"You are a savage, though I doubt you were born that way. You became one at the hands of your captors. Nothin' you did was right or can be excused. But this is a rough country, and people who survive have to become rough to do it. You are what you are, by choice or not, but you don't have to do what you did anymore.

"You got a Comanche heart and head, and I expect it will take quite a while for you to let go of the Injun in you. You won't have time enough to do it here. You're more likely to get sick and die on your own, or they'll eventually make up some excuse and hang you in spite of the rules.

"So this is my proposition. I've lived my life in rough country and in rough ways. Now I'm building a ranch in what used to be your backyard. So far, I'm the only one there, and I plan to use that position to get as much land as I can. I need help doing it, and nobody knows the canyons of the Llano like the Comanches.

"I'm offerin' you a deal. Come work for me. Stay with me, earn your keep, do honest work, and I'll stake you—a string of workin' ponies, grub, a roof to get out of the rain, boots, hat, and clothes to work in. After five years, you make the decision. You can stay with me, or I'll give you a place on the Middle Fork of the Red River and you can make your own way. I expect you'll be wantin' a place of your own and probably a woman."

The face across from him had not wavered, but it might have softened a bit.

"If you go back to the old ways, I'll hunt you down and kill you myself."

Goodnight spat again and leaned back in his chair. He had said what he needed. He sat.

The young man across from him remained silent. It was a full five minutes before he spoke. In a halting voice, a voice that was trying to remember a language mostly forgotten, he said, "I have...business. I have business in New Mexico. Then I come."

Goodnight spat again and leaned forward. "Well now, I thought so. I knew your dad, and I didn't like him. He was a corrupt and dishonest man who dealt badly with poor people, and he lacked integrity. I don't tolerate men who have no integrity.

"But the snake he was in cahoots with was worse, and your dad was treated without respect. Most of Las Vegas was just a dad-blasted den of vipers, but Hetley beat them all, and he deserved what he got.

"I reckon by now you know all the details of your father, your mother, and your sister, but it still leaves you as the owner of the house and the land. But you show up and people will know who you are, and you'll find your enemies numerous and powerful.

"Ending up in jail is no good, nor is dangling from a rope. You're too young. You been in the wild too much to sit behind bars and just die. That would be a waste. You may have been an Injun warrior, but you were a good one, and I respect that.

"In light of this situation, I have a second proposition. We'll get the range in order for the winter, and in the spring, I'll go with you to Santa Fe, where there's a better breed of people. I know someone who can help us get the deed and the will and do things legal. If you have more business than that, I'll ride on and leave you to finish it. You can catch up with me if you're still alive." He leaned back in the chair.

The young man remained silent for a couple of minutes and then nodded in agreement.

Tipton Mulvaney did not have many possessions. The school had taken what little he had, but they had agreed to store a quiver of arrows and a bow, a shield, and his buckskin clothes. He had never had a hat.

Mounted on the extra horse that Goodnight had brought, he sat almost a foot over the grizzled man beside him, his feet dangling beneath the stirrups. The superintendent held Goodnight's bridle for a moment longer.

"It won't work, Colonel," he whined. "He's a savage, you can't reform him. He's too set in his ways!"

Goodnight looked thoughtful for a moment and then spat. Dirt from the large wad of juice swirled up from the ground. "Well," he said, "that's what some people say about me."

The men turned the horses and hit a good trot toward the gate.

CHAPTER 23

PRESENT DAY

The Wednesday meeting of the Livestock Board postponed the final decision about the Buffalo Skull Ranch until the investigation could be finished. But the board did lift the quarantine and other restrictions, so the ranch was back in business.

The news of Lassiter Jones's involvement flashed around the art world, and the Museum of the American Cowboy was quick to disassociate itself from any dealings of its former director. The museum staff members, still at the hacienda, shocked and dismayed over their director's actions, adjourned and went home.

Bud was hesitant to reveal the secrets of Mulvaney Castle until more of the details could be worked out, but a Las Vegas newspaper broke the story. Nedra Hamilton was helpful to the reporters but eventually put off further discussion until she could, as a proper historian and possible heir to the house, study the issues further.

The Museum of New Mexico handled the recovery of everything in the upper room. The house, yards, corrals, and outbuildings were cordoned off until everything could be identified, recorded, and photographed, and soon, there was talk of declaring the house a historical site.

"If Tipton Mulvaney sent his sister the telegram," Mogi reasoned, "he must have done it when he and Goodnight were in Santa Fe. However he got connected to Charlie Goodnight, they both must have come to Santa Fe to settle the estate in 1879."

That was the second piece of paper. It was a legal document giving all of the shared inheritance of the Mulvaney properties and remaining monies to Lucy alone. It had been signed by Tipton and witnessed by a judge and Charles Goodnight.

"He settles the estate but knows that Lucy might never know about it. He goes to Las Vegas and sends the telegram, using a false name so he's not recognized. He writes it with as few words as possible, using the phrase that he knew Lucy, and only Lucy, would recognize. She would know to go to the chimney and go up to the hidden room."

"Then he goes to the castle." Jennifer took over telling the tale. "He guessed that his mother was in the upper room," she continued. "Remember how the maids swore she had never left the house? She hadn't. When they weren't looking, Violet Mulvaney opened a bookcase, entered the hidden stairwell, and went up to the room. She lived there for some time, probably. It was no ghost that people saw dancing on the porch —it was Violet in her wedding dress. Sometime later, she either starved to death or overdosed on a sleeping powder.

"Nine years later, in 1879, when Tip finds his mother's body in the room, he places the papers over her heart, where they will be easily found. He expects Lucy to get the telegram, understand what she must do, and then come soon, maybe within a few weeks. When she sends a telegram to him by way of Goodnight, he'll come get her, and they'll be a family again.

"But she doesn't see the telegram for forty-plus years. When she does finally read it, she realizes that her brother hadn't died, that he had survived his kidnappers. She realizes that he had gone back to the house and specifically written for her to join him. In that instant, she feels the injustice of her stepparents for hiding the telegram, the tragedy of not finding her brother, and the waste of all those years of living a life based on a lie. It hits her all at once, and she has a stroke or a heart attack or something, and dies."

Nedra opened the note and read it again. "I wonder how long he waited for her to contact him," she said quietly. "In his mind, he may have thought that she preferred the life in St. Louis and was no longer interested in having a brother. He may have thought that she chose not to come, that she had rejected him.

"If he had any heart left, her not coming home probably broke it."

————

Mogi and Jennifer sat relaxing with Granddad on the patio as the warmth of the morning sun began to dry out the air. Both had brought their belongings to the pickup and were ready to load up and leave. They were wishing that they could stay just a little longer.

Bud had opened up the swimming pool for the ranch staff and their families and had invited the band back for a special summer's end party. The calendar was already filling up with hacienda reservations. People kept asking if they could get a tour of Mulvaney Castle.

"It's been quite a summer for you grandkids," Granddad said as he stretched in preparation for the long drive back. "It's going to make school seem pretty dull."

"I was thinking about telling what I did for my summer vacation," Mogi said. "I saw a ghost, twice. I was led up a mesa by a century-old Indian who was also a ghost. I was run down by a glider flown by a guy who wore silver spurs and carried two Colt revolvers. I walked through and hid in a haunted house. I survived a flashflood. Oh, and I learned to be a cowboy and how to dance the two-step."

Jennifer laughed. "The last one is going to be hardest to believe."

Nedra Hamilton joined them at the table. "Well,

I'm getting a whole new level of fame," she said with a laugh. "I may have to break down and buy a computer so I can get people to write me instead of calling all day long on the telephone. I have so much to thank all of you for, and I have so little that I can give in return."

The Franklins assured her that they had been more than rewarded with the solving of the mysteries.

"I do, however," she continued, "have something that you might remember me by—something you might find very interesting." She reached into her briefcase.

"Before the museum staff loaded up and took off, one of them was already researching whether there was any proof that Tipton Mulvaney had worked for Charlie Goodnight in 1879. He had a book of photographs that had been taken around that period, so he looked for any that showed the cattle ranches around the Palo Duro Canyon.

"Goodnight started his first ranch in 1877, then moved over and started the most famous of his ranches, the JA, in 1878. He formed other ranches through the years, but his last one was his own, located a couple miles north of the rim of the Palo Duro. Putting his house there resulted in a town being built nearby that they named Goodnight, Texas.

"My friend left me his book, and I would like for you to have it. I know I can get a copy of my own through the university. Here, dear, page 76."

Professor Hamilton handed Mogi a large photography book that she had opened to a full-page photograph. The picture itself was one of a chuckwagon with a number of men sitting in a row along the ground in front, a few sitting on the wagon tongue, and several on horseback lined up behind the wagon. Written across the bottom in a white pen was *JA Roundup, 1881.*

The men looked remarkably similar, each wearing a long-sleeve shirt buttoned to the neck and suspenders or a vest. They wore a variety of hats— some tall, some short, most with flat brims, some slightly crushed, all looking well used. Their pants were dark, with most of the pant legs tucked into the tall tops of their boots. Some wore chaps.

The chuckwagon was stacked high with tied bedrolls, and several pieces of rigging for the horses lay scattered on the ground.

"Here," Nedra pointed.

Along the line of men on their horses in the back of the picture was a man much taller than the rest. His face was angular and gaunt. A large scar ran from his right ear up to his forehead. The hands folded over the saddlehorn were large, and his upper body was obviously broad-shouldered and thickly muscled.

But it was the eyes that drew Mogi's attention.

From beneath the brim of his hat, the man's expression appeared somber, his eyes singularly intense, as if he were seeing beyond the camera, beyond the camp, beyond the horizon to a place far away.

A LOOK AT: THE CAPTAIN'S CHEST

THE MOGI FRANKLIN MYSTERY SERIES 8

Unravel the Mystery and Survive the Storm in *The Captain's Chest*—An Action-Packed Middle-Grade Adventure!

A month in the Caribbean should be paradise—snorkeling, windsurfing, and dreaming of lost treasure from sunken ships. For fourteen-year-old Mogi Franklin, it's the perfect adventure. But when a friend vanishes without a trace, Mogi and his sister, Jennifer, stumble into a mystery more treacherous than the island's hidden reefs.

Their search for answers leads them into the depths of an international crime ring, where a powerful developer has sinister plans for the island of St. John. With a hurricane fast approaching and time running out, Mogi must rely on his instincts and problem-solving skills to uncover the truth before it's too late.

Blending thrilling action, family bonds, and the power of logic, *The Captain's Chest* is a heart-pounding installment in the *Mogi Franklin Mystery* series, perfect for middle-grade readers who love adventure, suspense, and fearless young heroes.

AVAILABLE MAY 2025

ABOUT THE AUTHOR

New Mexico-based Donald Willerton is the author of *Death in the Tallgrass*, the winner of the Western Writers of America 2024 SPUR Award for Western Historical Fiction, a finalist in the 2024 American Fiction Awards, and a finalist in the 2024 Storytrade Book Awards. He has written a ten-book Middle Grade/Young Adult mystery series located in the Southwest, two contemporary thrillers, and a fictional World War II adventure novel.

To finance his writing, he used his degrees in physics and computer science as a scientist, manager, and computer specialist, but has always let his curiosity, imagination, and passion for history keep his head aligned with his heart.